DIARY OF A STALKER

DIARY OF A STALKER

ELECTA ROME PARKS

URBAN
Renaissance

www.urbanbooks.net

Urban Books, LLC
1199 Straight Path
West Babylon, NY 11704

Diary of a Stalker copyright © 2010 Electa Rome Parks

ISBN-13: 978-1-60162-199-3
ISBN-10: 1-60162-199-X

First Trade Printing January 2010
Printed in the United States of America

10 9 8 7 6 5 4 3

This is a work of fiction. Any references or similarities to actual events, real people, living, or dead, or to real locales are intended to give the novel a sense of reality. Any similarity in other names, characters, places, and incidents is entirely coincidental.

Distributed by Kensington Publishing Corp.
Submit Wholesale Orders to:
Kensington Publishing Corp.
C/O Penguin Group (USA) Inc.
Attention: Order Processing
405 Murray Hill Parkway
East Rutherford, NJ 07073-2316
Phone: 1-800-526-0275
Fax: 1-800-227-9604

DEDICATION

To all who have helped keep my dream alive . . .

ACKNOWLEDGMENTS

I'm back! It has been over 2 years since my last novel dropped, I've had my ups and downs (don't we all?), but through it all, I survived. I didn't look back, arose triumphant and never stopped writing; it's ingrained in my spirit. And I didn't forget you—my loyal readers.

Thank you to all the readers who supported my previous works and who continued to e-mail and contact me via MySpace.com and Facebook.com, all asking the same question: *When is your next book coming out?*

Well, here it is. You are holding it in your hands. The wait is over! As usual, hold on tight for a wild, crazy ride. I so enjoy entertaining you guys and as always, I welcome your feedback. If you enjoy *DIARY OF A STALKER*, please spread the word—tell a friend or two or three (smile). Word of mouth sells books and this industry does not permit any half-stepping.

I'd be remiss if I didn't thank the following people who are forever believing in my talent, my dream, and me. Even when my faith falters, theirs never does. For that, I am forever grateful and always touched. Much love to my hubby, Nelson Parks; Brandon and Briana (my children); Tresseler Byrd, DaJuan Crooms, Jordan Rome, Laymon Taylor, Sharron Nuckles, Mardessa Smith and Leida Speller. I love you guys more than you'll ever know.

Special thanks goes out to my agent, Portia Cannon and to my new publishing family, Urban Renaissance. This is a new beginning . . . Let's make it happen. I'm a firm believer that everything happens for a reason.

To the online literary organizations that have promoted my books, thank you sincerely from the bottom of my heart:

APOOO, RAWSISTAZ, AALBC, Mosaic Books, The Grits, Disilgold.com, ChickLitGurrl, EDC Creations and Sormag. I realize I couldn't get the word out without you. You are the true literary ambassadors.

To the book club members (too many to name and you know who you are) who have welcomed me into your homes and hearts, much love and appreciation. You've warmed my heart with your unconditional support. I have enough wonderful memories to take me through another lifetime—all from women (and a few men) who embraced me with open arms. Didn't we have fun?

To my author friends: Cheryl Robinson, thank you for the many phone conversations and pep talks. You are one of the most positive people I've had the pleasure of knowing. Eric Pete, Cydney Rax, Mary Morrison, Marissa Monteilh and Darrien Lee: Thank you for the information sharing and being all around "good people."

If I have forgotten anyone, please charge it to my head and not to my heart. The dream lives on; in my heart and soul, and with God on my side, all things are possible. Amen. First, we have to ask for it, see it, and believe it. Then it will come.

Again, to my readers, I love you guys! But you already know that. Until our next journey together, peace and abundant blessings.

Much love,
Electa

P.S. E-mail your comments to novelideal@aol.com and keep track of what's going on in my world at www.electaromeparks.com, www.myspace.com/author_chick, www.electaromeparks.blogspot.com and facebook.com.

STALKING BEHAVIOR

- Watch
- Follow
- Harass
- Threaten
- Loiter
- Vandalize
- Assault
  - Physical
  - Sexual
  - Emotional
- Make unwanted telephone calls (land or cell phone)
- Send unwanted mail
- Leave unwanted gifts or packages
- Cyber Stalk:
  - Repeatedly e-mail
  - Impersonate in chat rooms, e-mails, or websites
  - Fraudulent online behavior

PROLOGUE

Darkness surrounded her with a thick cloak of protection, shadows bounced and ricocheted off the walls. She embraced it with open arms, like welcoming a long-lost friend back into the fold.

Silence. She felt safe now. While most people gravitated toward the light, she embraced the night, the cover of darkness. From experience, she knew that deeds not meant to be seen or heard were best carried out in the deep, secretive confines of the night.

Quietly and painfully slow, she crept out of the shadows, cautiously pushed clothes aside, opened the closed closet door and exited with precision. Her footsteps were deliberate and calculated. She knew every creak and crevice from memory. She walked with the confident stride of someone who was comfortable with her surroundings.

Ever so cautiously, she pushed the closet door open, just an inch. Stopped and listened. Then another inch. Then another. Silence, except for the even sound of breathing. She knew he was a deep sleeper, but she still didn't want to take any chance of him waking up. Tonight wouldn't be the night when she became careless. Even though she had been here before, numerous times, this was the first time with him being inside the house.

With the slinkiness and sneakiness of a feline stalking her prey, she moved from inside the closet to the master bedroom. Stopped just short of the massive bed and simply watched. Watched and reveled in the closeness they shared. Being in the same space with him thrilled her.

She had to force herself to breathe because he took her breath away. Every time. He did it for her. If only he would love her back. Even if it were only with a quarter of the love she felt for him . . . she'd still be satisfied. He slept on his back, breathing evenly, legs sprawled wide, with a thin sheet pulled up to his waist. She knew that underneath he was completely nude.

It took all she had not to reach out and touch him. She was so close, yet so far away. In her mind, he was absolutely perfect. Perfect for her. Her eyes eagerly and greedily took him in. Ravished him with her deep carnal yearning.

Why couldn't he simply love her back? This question played out in her mind over and over again, each and every day. Crippling her. Crushing her confidence. Making her crazy. Crazy like a loon. Sometimes she hated him. Hated him with a devastating passion. Those were the days she wanted to do something bad to him. Wanted to hurt him. Make him pay for not loving her.

Tonight, she simply watched. She stood there for hours and watched him peacefully sleep. If he had awakened and looked a few feet in front of him, he would have easily spotted her. Her desire to be near him overrode her fear of being caught.

Once she had her fill of him, she silently crept down the stairwell and out the front door, quietly closing it behind her. The next morning he would be none the wiser. Only the faint smell of her perfume would remain. He'd imagine he dreamt of a dark figure towering over him. Watching. And waiting. Waiting until it was time.

Chapter 1

PILAR

I'm your #1 fan.

It's funny how one's life can forever be changed with the utterance of four simple words: *I'm your #1 fan.* Well, actually, they weren't spoken, but sent to my favorite male author, Xavier Preston, by way of e-mail. *Man, I love the World Wide Web.*

I couldn't believe it; I had recently finished reading his latest national bestseller, *Secret Desires,* and to put it mildly, I was simply blown away. I felt like the main character was speaking directly to me, like she was inside my brain, picking it apart, piece-by-piece. I could relate to the storyline . . . totally . . . and the ending was spectacular, took my breath away. *Secret Desires* stayed with me, languishing inside my soul, like a sweet kiss that lingers into the early morning hours as dawn approaches.

Even though I am an avid reader—I should be since I'm a freelance writer—I typically do not contact authors about their books. I don't get caught up in the entire groupie side of the literary industry. Yes, it exists! Surprise, surprise! There is an entire circle of women all across the country, sometimes entire book clubs, who follow the lives and movement of African-

American male writers the same way groupies chase after rappers, rock stars, athletes and actors.

In the book industry, it is just a bit more subtle. For example, the book club president might fly the handsome, fine, articulate male author into her city for the weekend, to discuss his most recent hot release at the monthly book club meeting and to perhaps get the added bonus of getting up close and personal between the sheets. It happens.

For me, however, this was different; Xavier Preston made a lasting impression. And generally, it took a lot to impress me because I wasn't into the ordinary and I was determined to tell him how impressed I was. That is, after I went out and purchased all his previous novels. I had a bit of catching up to do.

A week later, after devouring his other six novels from cover to cover like a delicious gourmet meal, savoring every word, I knew I had to make contact. I simply had an unrelenting urge to speak with him. I couldn't get his lyrical, rhythmic, flowing words out of my head. This man moved me. Moved me like I had never been moved before. I felt a connection. A deep connection.

Early one morning, before I began writing an article for one of the local magazines I frequently wrote for, I e-mailed Xavier Preston my sincere, honest thoughts.

> Mr. Preston, I'm your #1 fan. I know you hear that all the time from readers, but I really, truly am. Your characters stay with me long after I've consumed the last page of your books. I never want your stories to end; they move me. You are super-talented, put these other authors to shame, and I'd love for you to autograph my books. By the way, I have all your novels. When will you be in Atlanta? A true, die-hard fan, Pilar.

Much to my surprise and pleasure, a couple of days later, I received a simple response.

Pilar, what a lovely name. Thank you for the sweet e-mail. I'm so pleased you've enjoyed my books over the years. I'd love to meet you as well. I enjoy meeting and greeting my readers. I will be signing at Medu Bookstore, at 5:00 P.M. next Saturday at Greenbriar Mall. Please, stop by if you get the opportunity. I would love to see you there. Xavier.

With a pounding heartbeat, I couldn't believe what I was reading and I re-read it a few more times for clarity. I wanted to make sure I was reading correctly that Xavier Preston asked to meet me. Me. Next weekend couldn't arrive soon enough.

It was Friday afternoon, a week after I had received Xavier's e-mail, and I was lying across my bed, admiring the author photo of Xavier on the back cover of his debut title, outlining his features with my index finger. He had such soulful, penetrating brown eyes and the sexiest pair of dimples I had ever seen. Such a handsome man. I was so caught up in looking at the picture that I almost forgot I had Leeda on the phone. Leeda and I had been friends since my days in Baltimore. I moved to Atlanta almost four years ago. Had to get out of Baltimore. Held too many memories, most of them bad.

"Pilar, for the life of me, I can't understand why you are so excited about meeting this author. My God, he's only an author. It's not like he's Jay-Z or Denzel," she exclaimed in her usual authoritative sounding voice, with a bit of amusement.

I sighed inwardly because Leeda didn't understand, or maybe couldn't understand, no matter how many times or how hard I tried to explain it to her.

"Xavier gets me. Period. He gets me. Read *Secret Desires* and you'll understand. It's as if he patterned the main character after me. Like he peeked inside my bedroom window and started writing. It's almost eerie. I have never met this man a day in my life, but it's like he reached inside my mind and penned my thoughts on paper."

"Pilar, there are many women who think exactly as you do. They are looking for a handsome soul mate and think there is only one true love for them. You aren't the only woman in the world who is a hopeless romantic. Your thoughts are not unique in that aspect."

Leeda could never understand, so I simply gave up trying to convince her that this was different. Xavier was different; I could feel it deep in my bones.

"Well, it won't hurt anything for me to attend the signing; after all, he did invite me. I can at least get my books autographed. Years from now, who knows, they might be very valuable."

"True. Just don't go there with expectations that are only in your mind," Leeda said.

"Whatever," I stated with an exasperated sigh.

"Pilar, don't get so defensive. You know how you are. We've discussed it before. Every man you meet who is kind to you is *not* the one. I don't want to see you hurt again."

"Please, let's not even go there," I said.

"Okay, if you say so. Just remember, life is what you make it. You don't need a man to make you whole."

"I know that, but I have a feeling that Xavier Preston is going to change my life for the better," I stated with a huge smile. I was on a natural high. A Xavier high.

Chapter 2

XAVIER

Never trust a big butt and a smile.

I've been in the literary game for several years now, with seven best-selling novels to my name. I figured out a long time ago that I have the gift of gab, of storytelling . . . and I love women. All shapes, sizes, colors and ethnicities. I don't discriminate; I believe in equal opportunity. Becoming a novelist was a natural progression seeing as how I've been telling tall tales my entire life. Women purchase most books, which is a good thing since my target market is definitely women, especially African American. If I depended on men for my livelihood, I would literally be a starving artist.

At this stage of the game, I have pretty much seen it all and done it all. If I must say so myself, I've led an exciting life. The stories I could tell. However, my "psycho bitch" radar must have been malfunctioning when this chick named Pilar first approached me. Damn, it leaves a sour taste in my mouth just to spit that bitch's name off of my tongue.

Never in a million years could anyone have told me that sweet face and banging body would spell trouble with a capital T. Never in a million years. I guess it's true . . . never judge a book by its cover. If I knew then what I know now, I would have pressed delete real quick when I received her very first e-mail.

"I'm your #1 fan!" Pilar didn't send an e-mail; she sent a virus, in the form of her very presence.

So sweet and accommodating—a boost to my already over-inflated ego, at least that's what I've been told. I received e-mails like that all the time from adoring female fans, so it never crossed by mind that inviting Pilar to my book signing would set my nightmare into motion, with my life quickly spiraling out of control and Pilar as the driver.

Even if I wrote the events that transpired into one of my novels, no one would believe them. They'd think Pilar was just a fabricated figment of my vivid imagination. Sometimes I think she is. I wake up hoping and praying that she is. However, I'm not that lucky.

I wish . . . I wish I could go back and rewrite the storyline, which is my life. Do some line editing and write that crazy-ass bitch out of the major scenes, hell the entire book. No, I'd kill her off in the first couple of chapters. Have her die a slow and torturous death. Yeah, that would make me happy. Very happy indeed.

Now, it's much too late for that. I have to deal with the consequences of my actions—or lack of. It's true—that line from an old Bell Biv Devoe song—*never trust a big butt and a smile.* I'm hardheaded. I had to learn the hard way.

Chapter 3

PILAR

It was on and poppin' . . .

As it quickly approached lunchtime on Saturday, I had probably changed outfits over three or four times. I had to look perfect. I finally decided on a pair of tight fitting designer jeans, the kind that made my butt look bootylicious and a colorful halter-top that showcased my ample breasts to the fullest. After slipping on my earth-toned platform shoes, I was set. Ready for the chase.

I had done my online research. The Internet was my best friend, and now I knew all about Xavier and his life story. I knew Xavier was tall, about six feet, two or three inches. At five feet six inches, I didn't want to appear to be too short when I first met him. I knew from experience that a lot of tall men didn't care for much shorter women. Plus, I wanted to be able to stare deep into those sexy brown eyes.

Even though I didn't live on that side of town, I had been out to Greenbriar Mall on a few occasions. I had even interviewed the store owner regarding their fourteen-year anniversary celebration for being in business, a couple of years back.

My timing was impeccable. I arrived at the signing fifteen

minutes before it was scheduled to end, with only two of his books in tow, Xavier's newest release and his very first title. The other books were strategically left in my car, on the front passenger seat. With me, everything had a purpose, a clear design.

When I casually sashayed to the bookstore entrance, I noticed most of the crowd was gone or dispersing and there were only two other women ahead of me in the line, waiting to meet the author. One was a middle-aged woman who was obviously a member of a book club, since she was dressed from head to toe in her purple-and-gold book club paraphernalia. The other reader was an absolute ghetto fabulous mess, complete with two-tone, brightly colored hair, nails with various designs and a dress so short and tight that if she bent over by one inch, Xavier would be staring at her ass crack. I think that was probably the plan.

At the entrance, the store owner had set up a table covered with an intricate African print tablecloth. Xavier's newest release, *Secret Desires*, was prominently displayed next to a beautiful floral arrangement that accented the colors from his cover. Next to the table was a huge overhead banner announcing the signing with a stunning photo of Xavier.

Behind the table stood the most gorgeous man my eyes had seen in a long, long time. My coochie automatically had a twitch, jerk reaction. I felt myself getting wet and I hadn't even said hello to the man yet. Unbelievable.

Xavier was tall, chocolate and sexy. A walking advertisement for sex; sex appeal gushed from his pores. And he was fine—had the type of body that made you wanna pinch yourself to make sure you weren't dreaming. His biceps were bulging from underneath the black T-shirt he wore tucked in black jeans. The only jewelry I noticed was an expensive-looking watch and a silver cross necklace.

When he opened his mouth and smiled, I saw a perfect set of white teeth, complemented by a pair of deep dimples, one in each cheek. Tall, dark and handsome . . . what a lethal combination. My coochie twitched twice this time and my nipples rose, hardened to show their appreciation. It's true that a woman knows within three minutes of meeting a man if she would sleep with him. With Xavier, it didn't take that long.

I continued to discreetly check Xavier out from behind the two talkative women ahead of me in line. He patiently answered their questions, made them feel special with his undivided attention. It didn't go unnoticed with me how he managed to make physical contact with them. A pat to the hand, a lingering touch to the shoulder, a hug. These women were eating it up. With his rugged, masculine looks, Xavier's aura screamed *this is a real man, the real deal!*

Xavier possessed a deep, sexy voice that gave me shivers as I imagined him whispering in my ear during a passionate make out session. I was simply mesmerized watching him in action, in his element. He carried himself with just the right mix of arrogance and swagger. The perfect combination. I could sense he was all man and used to wearing the pants in any relationship. Women catered to him, wanted to please him, so he would lavish them with his attention.

I caught myself checking out the huge bulge outlined in front of his jeans. From the size of his feet and hands, which didn't bear a wedding band, I was pretty confident he was packing. Packing some serious pipe. I shivered at just the thought and had no doubt that he knew how to use it.

When I glanced back up, our eyes briefly met. I realized I had been busted based on the slight amusement that shone in his dark eyes. My face flushed. Only one more reader to go before it was my turn to meet my favorite writer in the world. My hardened nipples betrayed my excitement.

Finally. It was my turn. Showtime.

"Hi, Mr. Preston," I said, stepping up and extending my right hand. "It is so great to finally meet you." I smiled sweetly.

"Please, please call me Xavier," he stated in a smooth, deep, rich voice that sent chills up and down my arms as he shook my hand in a firm grip, lingering a bit longer than necessary. His hand simply swallowed mine.

"Okay, Xavier," I said, getting used to the feel of his name as it rolled off my tongue. "I'm Pilar, the reader who e-mailed you a few days ago to tell you how much I've enjoyed your books. You're such a wonderful writer and your words stay with me long after the last page."

"Thank you so much. I appreciate your support, Pilar." He flashed that perfect smile and those deep dimples again. I wanted to fall into his arms and never let go.

"You invited me to come out and meet you, so here I am," I said, placing my hand on his upper arm for a couple of seconds.

"Oh, yes. I remember. How nice to meet you, Pilar. What a beautiful name for a beautiful woman," he flirted, staring into my eyes. I simply melted. I could have floated up to heaven at that moment.

"Thank you." I blushed as I inched a bit closer and made a point of bending down to place my two books on the table. I caught his eyes as they instantly shifted from my face to my chest. I knew he saw my dark, hardened nipples straining against the thin, sheer fabric of the halter. His lustful stare excited me.

"Would you mind autographing my two books? It would mean so much to me."

"Of course. Should I inscribe anything in particular?" he asked as he took a seat in the chair that was provided for him.

"No. Surprise me. I love surprises," I said in a flirty, seductive tone as I traced my finger across the outer edge of the front of the tablecloth.

Xavier looked at me curiously for a few seconds. Like he wanted to say something but changed his mind. I watched intently as he proceeded to sign my books in a bold, crisp, loopy handwriting with a black Sharpie marker. Being so up close and personal made me desire him even more. The mixture of his woodsy cologne and natural body odor was masculine, appealing and very alluring. I boldly held his eye when he looked back up to hand me my books.

"Thank you again. This means so much," I said, reaching for them, and my finger accidentally rubbed against the side of his hand. Two quick feather-like strokes followed.

"You are very welcome," he said and smiled. Those dimples stood out again.

"Would it be all right if I took a photo of us together? My friends won't believe it when I tell them I actually met and talked to author extraordinaire, Xavier Preston."

"Anything for you, Pilar," he stated in a tone that implied sexual overtones. "I have never been able to say no to a beautiful woman."

I blushed.

I quickly caught the attention of one of the store employees, who gladly came over and snapped a photo of us with my digital camera. It was a perfect moment in time. Forever captured . . . me with the biggest smile on my face, grinning like a Cheshire cat, Xavier's arm wrapped protectively around my waist, not an inch of space between us. A perfect moment.

All too soon, we pulled apart and I said my goodbyes as the store owner whisked him away to a back room to sign the few remaining copies of his book. I walked around the store, not really looking for anything in particular. I already had several books on my nightstand that were screaming for me to finally read them. They had been there for over a month gathering dust. Now, I was simply biding my time, setting up the second half of my well thought out plan.

After I looked at some cute postcards, just as I was flipping through some magazines, Xavier stepped from the backroom and proceeded to tell everyone goodbye as he made his exit. I waved shyly and continued to act as if I was caught up in reading an article from an entertainment magazine. After he left, I slowly counted to ten before I followed behind.

When I turned the left corner out of the store, I didn't immediately see him. My heart sank. Then I saw him leaving the nearby Chik-fil-A with a bottled water in hand, heading toward the exit. Xavier had a confident, long stride with his head held high. I saw women checking him out and whispering.

I briskly strolled and caught up with him just as he was opening the door to walk outside.

"We meet again," I said as he held the door open for me.

"Yes, we do."

He smiled.

I smiled back.

We were now standing outside on the sidewalk. "Could I ask you a huge favor? I know you are busy and all and I don't want to take up your precious time, but . . ."

"Pilar, Pilar. What's the favor?" he asked, slightly amused.

"Remember I told you that I had all your books? Well, I know a lot of stores have a two book limit at signings, and I didn't want to carry them all in to be turned away. But, I have the others in my car. Would you be able to sign those as well? To save time, you don't have to write anything; your signature is fine."

"Remember what I told you in the store? For you, anything. Lead the way."

As I led the way to my red convertible, it was on and popping. If things went as planned, I would be waking up in Xavier Preston's bed Sunday morning. With him fully satisfied. I loved it when a plan came together.

Chapter 4

XAVIER

If it walks like a duck, quacks like a duck, looks like a duck . . .
Okay. I readily admit it . . . I'm a dog. *Bow Wow.* As I said
before, like Sampson from the Bible whose weakness was his
hair, my weakness is a good-looking woman. Pilar is a gorgeous, smooth brown–skinned Georgia Peach with wild, spiral
curled, flyaway hair. With big doe-shaped eyes, melt in your
mouth C-cups and a round, firm ass that I could picture sitting
on top of my swollen dick, I knew I'd let her lick my lollipop.

I admit it. Pilar turned me on with that first smile. I'm not
naïve by any means when it comes to women, and I knew she
was checking me out, flirting, and trying to get my attention. I
thought it was cute. Little did she know, she had my attention
the minute I saw her walking up.

I had witnessed this scenario all before, played out with different women, in different cities. All gushing about how much
they loved my books as they accidentally, *yeah right*, rubbed
their breasts up against my arm. Sometimes, I said thank you
for your support and went on my way, but other times, I
wanted to hit it and quit it for a night. Notice I said for a
night. Typically, I was not a repeater—I didn't come back for

seconds. I didn't want to give any false illusions to these women who shared my bed on my book tours. It was what it was . . . a one-night stand, nothing more, nothing less.

Pilar and I ended up back at my hotel, The Ritz Carlton in Buckhead. She left with me after securing her car, and we had dinner and several drinks at one of the trendy restaurants in that popular area. I love Atlanta. It is one of my favorite cities, mainly because of the rich African-American culture it possesses and of course, the beautiful women. Usually when I arrived in Atlanta, I typically rented a car and didn't rely on a car service with a guide that my publishing house provided in other cities. I enjoyed having my own vehicle in Atlanta with the ability to come and go as I pleased.

Dinner was nice and relaxing, which was exactly what I wanted because I needed to unwind. Conversation was light, not too deep. I did most of the talking. The more drinks we consumed, the more comfortable Pilar and I became with each other. She was very intelligent, articulate and not the run of the mill type of chicks that typically threw themselves at me. Sexual tension filled the air. Could have sliced it with a steak knife.

I knew it was time to pay the bill and make a quick exit when she leaned over and whispered in my ear, "When are you going to take me back to your room and fuck me?"

I almost choked on the last swallow of my gin and tonic. This was a woman after my heart. She knew what she wanted, and was upfront and direct with it. No bullshit games. Aggressive was her middle name. Needless to say, we didn't hang around at the restaurant much longer after that.

The drive back to the hotel was full of sexual overtones. The air inside the car sizzled and cracked with the sexual vibes that girl was putting out. At one point, Pilar reached over and literally grabbed and stroked my dick through my jeans. I almost came then and there, on the spot. Especially when she leaned over and seductively licked the side of my face and ear

with her tongue. Her perfume was intoxicating. Pilar was intoxicating.

"I can't wait to taste your dick," she whispered in my ear. "I
bet you'd like that."

"You wanna suck my dick, baby?"

"Can't wait. I bet it's sweet as sugar."

"What do you know about that?" I kidded with her. "Most
women don't know how to bring it correct. I end up teaching
them how to please me. And if they finally get it right, then
they don't want to swallow."

"They don't know what they're missing," she stated as she
gently stroked me through my jeans and licked her lips in a seductive gesture. She had the art of seduction down to a science.

"Don't worry, I'll take good care of you and big daddy," Pilar
said, looking up at me with those big eyes.

I thought I had died and gone to heaven. This chick was a
straight freak. She had a sweet, innocent face, but she was definitely straight "anything goes." I sent a silent thank you up to
heaven and thought, *this is why I love Atlanta.* I love the ATL.

Three, four hours later, I had literally lost track of time after
hours of screwing. Pilar and I were laying in my bed, under the
crisp, cool sheets. She had her head resting on my chest and
was completely exhausted, knocked out in full sleep mode.
Pilar did not disappoint. She did exactly what she said she'd
do, suck dick like she knew exactly what she was doing.

I had an out of body experience several times. Had me
moaning, crying out like a little girl, twisting, and trying to get
away from her grasp when I couldn't possibly come again. Pilar
enjoyed it rough. As delicate as she appeared, she wanted me
to take her forcefully. Begged me to screw her hard. I had
learned that some women loved rape fantasy sex. The idea of
being forced to fuck turned them on. I could role-play with the
best of them.

"Oh, babe, give me all that big, juicy dick," she screamed.

"This how you want it?"

"Oh, yes! Give me all that dark meat. Oh yeah, go deeper, babe."

"Like this?" I asked in mid-stroke. I was literally putting my back into it. Wanted her to feel my every stroke.

"Harder! Deeper, babe!" she screamed, rising up to meet me in mid-stroke.

"You like that? Answer me. You like that?"

"More, give me more. Yesss! I can't get enough of you," she moaned softly.

"Spread your legs wider for me," I told her.

I didn't hold back; I gave it all to her. Pilar eagerly and greedily took it. I'm not bragging about my skills or my size, but I'm not your average dude in dick size. Most women can't take all of me at once. They have to get a few inches at a time, until they get used to me filling them up to the brim. As for the skills, let's just say that I know how to bring it correct. I've never, ever had a woman leave my bed unsatisfied.

At one point she was on her hands and knees, with her ass hoisted up in the air, literally offering herself to me. I laid the pipe and laid it well.

"Spank me, babe."

"What?" I asked, not surprised at all. Pilar was a freak.

"Spank my ass!"

I obliged and lightly tapped her butt with my open palm. Two taps, one on each side of her buttocks. I didn't want to hurt her.

"Harder. I'm not fragile."

I smacked her ass again.

"You can't do better than that?" she asked, wiggling her cheeks back and forth, teasing me. I'm an ass man, so that turned me on big time.

I gave her exactly what she asked for. Pilar wanted to feel the sting of pain. I sensed pain turned her on. She didn't have to ask me twice. Between my hand slapping her buttocks and my tool pumping deeply in and out of her, I couldn't tell if she was moaning in pain or pleasure. At some point, it meshed together into one big orgasm. She came hard, several times. I felt her come streaming down my thigh.

I loved watching her come. Her eyes would roll back in her head, she'd moan and make deep guttural sounds like it felt so good to her, her legs would start shivering, she'd reach for me and then let go, with her face buried in my neck until her heavy breathing subsided. Afterwards, she'd lay there with this totally satisfied expression on her face, like I had taken her to heaven and back.

Later, she was lightly snoring, curled up next to me, happy as a lark with her head on my chest. I pushed her wild hair out of her face. I watched her sleep for a few minutes and she looked like she didn't have a care in the world. Pilar was a beautiful woman. Her physical appearance, though striking, still betrayed the freak she was behind closed doors. I didn't know if she had a boyfriend or not, but if she did, he was one happy, lucky man. I wished my fiancée had her skills.

Yes, I did say fiancée! In my defense, I can say I hadn't had a rendezvous on the road in a very long time. I had definitely toned it down, preparing for when I would marry and be totally faithful to the love of my life. I had definitely sown my wild oats over the years, sown them well, and knew I had found a woman I could settle down with and start a family. Pilar was just a momentary lapse of judgment on my part.

She moved in her sleep, turned her backside to me, and the sheet fell away from her toned, taut body. I admired it. I couldn't resist stroking and caressing her ass as she unconsciously pressed it against my thigh. I changed position so that I was spooning with her, my arm around her tiny waist.

This gave me the freedom to touch and tweak her nipples with my right hand. In no time, they were erect and swollen. I played with them between my thumb and forefinger. Pilar moaned softly in her sleep. I stopped. Waited for her to settle back down. Didn't want to wake her. Spreading her legs with my hand, I inserted a finger into her pussy. Damn, she was still wet. I inserted another finger and dove deep, moving in and out. Very slowly. I didn't want to wake her, not yet anyway. I wanted to enjoy the sensation of her wetness and warmth. My dick rose to the occasion in record time.

This chick's body did something to me. She physically possessed everything I enjoyed in my women: a pretty face, a tight ass, ample breasts with thick nipples and good pussy. Yeah, I was definitely going to hit it a couple more times before I paid a taxi to take her back to her car tomorrow morning. There was no shame in my game.

Chapter 5

PILAR

The morning after . . .

The next morning, I woke to the delicious smell of scrambled eggs and crisp bacon. Xavier was so sweet and thoughtful; he had taken the liberty of ordering breakfast. He carried the tray over to the bed and fed me a forkful of eggs, after planting a full kiss on my lips. He tasted minty and fresh.

"Good morning, sleepyhead."

"Good morning," I stated. "What time is it?" I asked, yawning, covering my mouth with the back of my hand.

"It's almost ten."

"Really?" I asked, propping myself up on the fluffy bed pillows.

"Really," he stated, pushing my hair out of my face. I knew it was probably all over my head, making me look like a wild, unkempt woman.

"I'm sorry . . . It's this medication I take. Makes me sleepy."

"Don't be. After the workout you put in last night, you deserve to sleep as long as you like."

I blushed.

"Eat up," he said, pointing to the tray that was placed next to me.

"Okay. You aren't eating anything?" I asked, as I looked at the scrambled eggs, crisp bacon, buttered toast, and fresh squeezed orange juice arranged on a silver tray with a single red rose in a pretty crystal vase.

"No. I ate earlier, downstairs. While you were still knocked out to the world."

"Oh."

"I'll just grab a glass of orange juice," Xavier said.

"Sure. Help yourself."

"You know I'm out of here in a few hours. Have to head back to the airport. Fly back home to Houston."

"Oh, I thought we would be able to spend today together," I stated with obvious disappointment. I pouted. Didn't look at him.

"No. I'm out of here, cutie. Only flew in for a couple of days."

"I see," I stated in a pitiful voice. "I didn't really get to talk to you like I wanted to. We were too busy doing other things."

Xavier shrugged like it didn't matter to him. "Listen, I'm going to run downstairs to the gift store for a few minutes and pick up some batteries for my MP3 player. Why don't you finish eating, take a hot shower and meet me back here in thirty minutes?" he stated, patting the bed. "I'll place the DO NOT DISTURB SIGN on the door handle."

Xavier didn't wait for my response. He simply kissed me on the lips and walked out the door. I looked around and noticed he took his cell phone with him, which spoiled my plan of getting his number.

I ate a little more of my breakfast, found my purse in a chair and popped a pill while I was thinking about it, then I went into the bathroom to freshen up. When Xavier came back to the room thirty minutes later, I had followed his instructions. I was buck-naked and waiting underneath the sheets.

Xavier didn't say a word. Pulled down his running shorts,

stripped off his T-shirt and climbed under the sheets, with his big-ass dick pointing in my direction. The sight of him in the buff took my breath away all over again.

"Get over here and suck some dick," he commanded playfully, pulling on my arm.

"No. Wait."

"No?" he asked, surprised.

"That's what I said," I announced playfully, pulling away.

"Come on, Pilar. You know how you like sucking on this. You couldn't get enough last night," he stated, stroking it up and down in his hand.

He continued to gently stroke my cheek and hair with his other hand, whispering to me. "Come on, baby. I'm leaving for Houston soon and you do that shit too good. Give me something to remember you by."

"What are you going to do for me?" I asked, stroking his chest, circling his tattoo, the one over his heart, with my finger.

"Come here. Quit playing," he stated, attempting to pull my head down into his lap. "Suck it."

I resisted again and he finally realized that I was very serious, too.

"You know what? I probably should get to the airport as early as possible. Wouldn't want to miss my flight. I'm going to get the concierge to get a taxi to take you back to your ride," he said, already dismissing me.

"You aren't driving me back?"

"No, I won't have time," he said with annoyance.

"It's still early. You don't have to leave yet, do you?"

I looked down at his erect dick. I knew he was telling me in no uncertain terms that if I wanted to stay with him a while longer, I had better get on my knees and start sucking. I had already figured out that he liked me in a submissive position so he could watch me. Plus, Xavier liked to play with my breasts as I sucked him off.

An hour later, I had given a blowjob to die for and now he was about to come again as I rode him like a rodeo cowgirl. Hmm, he felt so delicious. He wouldn't forget me anytime soon.

Thirty minutes later, he was opening the back door to a taxi and giving the African driver the address to Greenbriar Mall. Xavier bent down, kissed me on the cheek. I pulled him back by the shirt collar and kissed him full on the lips, forcing my tongue into his mouth. He accepted it and sucked.

After a few moments, he pulled away. He said, "Thank you," right before he closed the back door and the driver sped off.

I glanced out the passenger window, to see Xavier's back as he strolled back into the hotel. All I could think was, *After all we did last night, all he can say is thank you.*

Chapter 6

XAVIER

Can I have my cake and eat it too?
I love my life. I'll say that again: I love my life.

After a highly successful twelve-city book tour, I was back home, in my hometown of Houston, born and raised here. Wouldn't trade it for anywhere. Used to do some crazy, thug-ass shit in these streets. Man, the stories I could tell. Who knows? Maybe one day I would write about my experiences. After I decided to make something out of myself years ago, I had since stayed away from all illegal activities that consumed my youth.

After recuperating most of Sunday, Monday morning I was energized, ready to begin work on another project. I've been blessed to be a full-time writer. Writing pays my bills and keeps my lights on. I count my blessings every day because I know it easily could have been a very different story. I could have been doing a bid in somebody's prison, just another black male statistic.

I take my job and craft very seriously and I'm a stickler for rigid schedules. I get up bright and early every morning, usually around six o'clock, rain or shine and work out for an hour.

By seven-fifteen, I'm usually showered and dressed for the day. I may read the paper for half an hour, after I've cooked breakfast. By 8:00 A.M., I am signing onto my computer, ready for a full day of writing, editing, promoting and responding to e-mails regarding literary events and paid speaking engagements.

Depending on my creativity, I may work until 5:00 or stop around lunchtime and spend the rest of the day watching movies, good movies. I'm a certified movie addict and have an extensive collection that I'm proud to show off.

My one pet peeve: I don't allow my friends and relatives to disrespect my craft. Just because I work from home, occasionally from Starbucks, doesn't mean they can call me up and chat or send me frivolous e-mails throughout the day. I don't have time for that shit.

First of all, I am not a phone person (I don't enjoy talking on the phone for endless hours about endless nonsense) nor do I like e-mailing back and forth all day. I have much better things to do with my valuable time. Anyone who knows me, knows these things are big no-nos. No if, ands, or buts, I don't tolerate distractions from anyone.

Around lunchtime Monday, I had had a very productive day; I considered ten usable pages as being productive. I was feeling good and ready to check out a movie for a couple of hours, just chill out and relax. Perhaps drink a beer. Just as I was getting ready to sign off, I heard the familiar *you've got mail* announcement.

Clicking into my AOL account, I saw the following e-mail:

> Hey, babe. I really enjoyed this weekend; hope you did, too. I miss you already and can't stop thinking about you and the things we did. Electric. Chat back.

I smiled and my tool instantly became rock hard. Yeah, I'm not going to lie. I had thought about Pilar a few times since I returned to Houston. Hell yeah. Had me crying out like a little bitch while she went down on me. Damn right, I had thought about her. She tripped me out Sunday morning though. It was odd how she went from hot to cold. Saturday night, she was serving her pussy up on a platter, but Sunday morning I pretty much had to beg her to spread her legs for me. Strange.

I e-mailed her back.

> Hey, you. I enjoyed meeting you Saturday. Again, thanks for your support and making for a memorable Atlanta trip.

Pilar must have been waiting by her computer, because seconds later I received another e-mail.

> Do you miss me? I miss you.

I'm thinking, *What the fuck? Do I miss her? I don't even know her. What kind of sixth grade shit is this?*

I quickly sent my response.

> Again, thank you for a great night. Gotta run. Take care.

I waited a few seconds, just in case she decided to respond again. Thankfully, she didn't. If she had e-mailed me several times in the middle of my writing time, I would have been seriously upset. Nah, let's keep it real; I wouldn't have been upset, I would have been pissed. Pilar did not want to witness me pissed.

A few moments later, my cell phone rang. I smiled when I saw the number that I knew from memory.

"Hey, baby."

"Hey to you," Kendall purred.

"What's up? How's your day going?" I asked, with all thoughts of Pilar immediately gone. Pilar who? No one compared to my baby.

"It's going all right. Better now that I'm talking to you," she cooed.

"That's what I like to hear, baby girl."

"You were so tired yesterday that you never told me how your trip to Atlanta went."

I lied easily. "Nothing special. Same ole, same ole. Once you've done one signing, you done them all."

"I was just wondering. Usually when you come home from a road trip, you want me waiting in your bed."

"And I still want that . . . tonight. Yesterday, I was dead tired. Remember I'm coming off a twelve-city tour. That's not easy. It takes a toll on a person's body."

"I know. Poor baby. You need some tender loving care, just some good ole TLC," she said in a baby-like tone.

"Are you coming over tonight? I'll even cook for you." Suddenly, I realized how badly I wanted to see her.

"Do you want me to?" she asked.

"What did I tell you about answering a question with a question?"

"Whatever, man. Yeah, I'll be there. After school and study time. Around seven."

"I'll be here."

"You better be. I want you all to myself," Kendall said.

"You got me, baby. I'm all yours. Wouldn't have it any other way."

"And you know it. I love you."

"Ditto. See you soon."

Yes. I love my life. Absolutely love it.

Chapter 7

PILAR

Time for Plan B . . .

"I know you are dying to tell me how the signing went," Leeda said.

"It was fabulous," I said in a dreamy, far away voice.

"A signing was fabulous? That's an odd way to describe it."

"Well, not necessarily the signing. It was okay. What was fabulous was what happened afterwards."

"And what happened afterwards?" Leeda questioned.

"I hooked up with Xavier Preston," I stated nonchalantly.

"Pilar, what does that mean? You hooked up with Xavier Preston?"

"What do you think it means? I slept with him."

"Pilar, you didn't."

"Leeda, I did," I said sarcastically.

"Do you really want to be used like that?" she questioned.

"I wasn't used. I wanted him to fuck me, and he screws very well, by the way. If anything, I used him. I got what I wanted, several times."

"I honestly think it was a huge mistake," Leeda said.

"Whatever. I don't care. You can never be happy for me."

"Calm down. I do want you to be happy, but sleeping with Xavier Preston isn't going to bring you happiness; temporary pleasure, but not happiness."

"How do you know, Leeda? You don't even know the man," I questioned.

"And neither do you, Pilar. Think about it. You don't know him; you just slept with him."

"I intend to solve that problem. Soon, I'll know him very well, if things go as planned," I murmured under my breath.

"What? I didn't hear you."

"Oh, nothing. I didn't say anything," I said with a sneaky grin on my lips.

"I have to go, but we'll talk next week. Call me if you need me," Leeda said.

"I will. Take care."

"You too. I worry about you. Please take care of yourself."

"Don't. I have everything under control now."

"Actions speak louder than words," Leeda said.

"And you'll see. I promise. I always wind up on top."

"That you do. That you do." With that said, Leeda disconnected our call.

I pushed the end call button on my cordless phone and tossed it across my bed. Sometimes, talking to Leeda simply exhausted me. Drained me. She thought she knew everything, and that constantly got on my nerves. She did everything right. I, on the other hand, could never get it right, according to her. But she had been there for me during the hard times, and that was what counted. Actions speak louder than words.

I was dead serious about finding out more about Xavier. This wasn't over yet. It wasn't over until I said it was. It didn't get past me that Xavier didn't say he missed me. I incorrectly assumed that the off the chain sex would keep me on his mind. Wrong! Wrong! Wrong!

Now, it was time for plan B. I had learned to always have a

backup plan in life. I'd already determined, by checking out his website, he was going to be back in Atlanta for some sort of annual conference in another month. In fact, Xavier was one of the featured authors.

It was an event called the National Book Club Conference, where authors and avid readers from all across the country converged on Atlanta for a weekend. I had plans to attend and interview a few authors and book club members for a magazine article I intended to write.

With a contented smile on my face, I lay back down and fell into a dream-filled sleep. In my dream, Xavier was thrilled at seeing me again at the conference. He confessed how he hadn't been able to get me off his mind since the last time we were together. Xavier and I spent the entire weekend together when he wasn't at the conference. In the dream, we talked, had serious conversations, made love. This time around we didn't fuck; this time, we made love. By the time he left for Houston, he realized he couldn't live without me.

Chapter 8

XAVIER

The love of my life . . .

As Kendall strolled into the house and closed the door, I met her with a deep open mouth kiss and held her close for a few moments, breathing her in. She felt so good in my arms; the perfect fit.

"You need to go away more often if I'm going to be greeted with this type of reunion kiss on your return." Kendall laughed.

"You look beautiful, as always."

"Thank you. Always for you, sweetie," she said, walking further into the living room and linking her arm through mine.

"I'm starving," she said, glancing in the direction of my kitchen. "What's for dinner?"

"I am too," I said, nuzzling her neck and running my fingers through her shoulder length black hair. I rained light kisses from the top of her slender neck down to her small breasts. She moaned a little but gently pushed me away.

"I'm starving for food, sweetie. It's been a long, hard, studious day. You said you'd cook dinner for me. Remember?"

"Did I?" I asked, scratching my chin. "I don't remember telling you that."

"Yes, you did," she said, punching me lightly on the arm. "Stop playing."

"My baby is studying hard in law school, isn't she?"

"You're damn right. Law school is no joke and I had been out of undergraduate for a few years before I went back to school. It's kicking my butt," she laughed. "We can't all sit around creating fictional characters for a living, existing in a fantasy world."

"Wait a minute. Hold up! Are you trying to say I don't work hard for a living?"

"No, sweetie, not at all. I just meant . . ."

I gently kissed her on the lips. "Baby, I was just messing with you. I know what you meant." Sometimes Kendall cracked me up because she could be so naïve.

I saw relief immediately register on her pretty face.

"Well, come on, mademoiselle. Your scrumptious meal awaits."

I took her hand in mine and led her into the kitchen, pulling out her chair so she could sit comfortably.

"My baby has had a hard day, but don't fret. Later I'll knock out all the kinks and hook you up right."

"Xavier."

"What?"

"I don't like for you to be so crude," she said slightly frowning.

"That wasn't being crude. I didn't say I couldn't wait to fuck you after we eat," I said, annoyed now.

She cringed.

As much as I loved Kendall, that was the one thing she had to work on. For someone so young, she could be prudish at times. I didn't exactly blame her. She had a pretty sheltered upbringing. Went to private schools; wasn't exposed to the real world. Her parents kept a tight rein on her and instilled the importance of acting like a lady at all times. Sex was okay between us, but it could be better. I was working on it, taking it slow, but there were still some things I couldn't get her to do with me or to me behind closed doors. That was a problem be-cause sometimes I wanted to get downright freaky.

When Kendall first met me and agreed to dinner after I spoke at her university as a guest author, she didn't know what to make of me. I always kidded with her that she had never met a real nigga until me. I keep it real. Always.

"Sweetie, this was delicious." We had finished off baked chicken, brown rice and green beans with a couple of glasses of wine.

"It never ceases to amaze me how you can throw down in the kitchen."

"And let's not forget the bedroom."

Kendall laughed easily.

"Seriously, growing up in a single parent home, with a mom who worked two jobs, you'd better learn how to cook or starve."

"Well, the least I can do is place the dishes in the dish-washer," Kendall stated, rising from the table, gathering plates and silverware.

"No. Don't worry about that. Leave them."

"You sure?"

"Yes, I'm sure. I have dessert waiting for you upstairs."

"Do you now?" she asked, with a slight smile on her lips.

I stood up, came around to her side of the table and took her hand. "Follow me and I'll show you."

When we made it upstairs to my master bedroom, Kendall gasped with joy and surprise.

"Oh, sweetie! This is beautiful. You are so romantic. I just love you so much," she said, kissing me lightly on the lips.

Earlier, I had slipped into the bedroom and lit dozens and dozens of red and white candles, her favorite colors, sorority colors and my fraternity colors. There were red rose petals leading from the entrance of my bedroom, up to my bed. Soft music was piped into my surround sound system, setting the mood.

"Thank you. I love this. The dinner, and this, it's wonderful. You are so good to me. You spoil me. Treat me like a princess."

"I have one more surprise."

"Really? What? There's more?"

I walked over to the walk-in closet and pulled out a box wrapped in silver paper with a big red bow.

"What's this?" she asked, excitement in her voice.

"Why don't you open it and find out," I stated, watching her every move.

Kendall took the box and walked over to my bed. Inside the box was a sexy red teddy. I knew Kendall would look beautiful wearing it the minute I saw it in the store.

"Go put it on and model for me, baby."

"This is totally see through. Leaves nothing to the imagination," she said, holding it up, inspecting it.

"And? Most lingerie is, baby. Did you want me to get you some thick flannel grandma-looking shit?"

"I'd feel uncomfortable walking around in this," she said in a near whisper.

I glanced around the room like I was looking for someone else.

"The only person up in here, besides yourself, is me, your man." For the second time that evening, I tried to hide my annoyance.

"I know, sweetie. You're right. I'm acting silly. Of course, I'll model it for you. It's beautiful and so thoughtful of you to take the time to pick it out."

"I thought it'd look sexy on you, not that it's going to stay on for very long."

Kendall took the teddy into the bathroom and returned a few minutes later. She took my breath away. I lay back on my bed, with my hands behind my back, and admired her. Everyone who knew us said we made a stunning couple.

"You are beautiful," I said, standing up and twirling her around for a better look. I didn't realize how much I missed making love to her. I had been gone for two and a half weeks on tour. Kendall and I hadn't spent a lot of time together lately because of my schedule. Plus, her studies took up a great deal of her free time.

"Thank you. I feel beautiful."

"Come here. Lay down on the bed."

She obliged and curled up on the bed. It always amused me how shy she'd get when we were about to make love. We had dated now for over a year, got engaged two months ago and I had made love to her too many times to count. Yet, she always acted like it was our first time. Sometimes, I wanted her to be more aggressive, tell me what she liked, what she wanted me to do to her. Be more like Pilar. *Hell, where did that come from?* Kendall would simply lie there and let me do all the work. However, all that was going to change.

"I've missed you so much," I proclaimed, kissing her neck.

"Have you?"

"What have I told you about answering a question with a question?" She had a bad habit of doing that all the time. Irritated the hell out of me.

"You missed me?" I asked.

"Of course, sweetie."

"Show me."

She blushed.

"Show you how?"

I tapped her forehead. "Are you sure you are a grown-ass woman of twenty-eight? I know I don't have to show you how to please your man," I joked, running my hand through her hair.

I had disrobed and climbed on the bed to straddle her. I gently kissed her neck and face, as my hands roamed down to her breasts. She moaned and closed her eyes.

"Kendall, open your eyes."

"Why?"

"I want you to look at me when I make love to you. I want to be staring into your beautiful eyes when you come."

"Okay."

"Now, get on your knees and come over here and suck some dick."

"What?"

"You heard me. Suck my dick."

"Sweetie, you know I don't know how to do that very well."

"I'll teach you."

"I don't like doing that."

"You aren't doing it for you. You are doing it because it pleases me," I said a little too forcefully.

She turned her head to the side, looking away from me.

"Kendall, don't act like this is the first time we've talked about this."

"I know," she said, looking up at me. "I want to satisfy you, please you. Honestly I do, but not when you treat me like a whore."

"How is that treating you like a whore? I'm just asking you to try. Okay?" I asked, stroking her breasts in firm circular motions, relaxing her.

"Okay. I'll try."

As my fingers slowly pulled the straps of the teddy off her shoulders, my mouth instantly went to her nipples, from one to the other. Back and forth, back and forth. When they were good and erect, I bent down and sucked as I slowly eased a finger inside her, then another. That caused an instant reaction. Believe it or not, all it took for me to get my baby off was for me to finger fuck her with two fingers and to suck and lick her breasts. That got her completely off . . . and she loved it. Lately, she even enjoyed me eating her out; at first, she thought it was nasty. Now, she couldn't wait for me to go down.

With all that, she still refused to suck my dick or let me do her doggy style. Claimed my dick was so big that it hurt her when I entered her from behind. Said it felt like it was coming out her stomach.

I manually stimulated her for a few more minutes and bent down to lick her clit. She moaned and lifted her ass up off the bed to meet my mouth.

"How does that feel?"

She moaned again.

I massaged her clit with one finger and eased two fingers into her pussy. Kendall's eyes glazed over in ecstasy.

"Does that feel good?"

She shook her head.

"I don't know what that means. How does it feel?" I asked, a bit gruff.

She didn't say anything. I stopped. We lay there looking at each other, Kendall's breathing evening out.

"Sweetie, why did you stop?"

"I asked you how it felt. I need you to talk to me. Let me know what turns you on."

"I feel embarrassed saying those things to you."

"Baby, how many times have I told you that it is just you and me behind closed doors? We should be able to do whatever we want to each other, say whatever we want to each other. We are two consenting adults."

"I know, but you are the first *real* man I've been with. The others were just boys trying to get off, not caring if I did or not," she said, massaging my back.

"Well, this is what most real men want: for you to talk dirty during sex, instead of just laying there like a limp doll."

"I'm not used to . . ."

"Well, baby, get used to it."

Kendall didn't utter a word.

"Did you hear me?"

"Yes. I hear you. I don't understand why you are being so mean to me. This started out as a great evening."

"I don't mean to sound harsh and I'm not being mean. I just

want you to be the best and to give of yourself in bed. That's all," I said very gently. "I want us to be able to please each other to the maximum."

"I'll try."

"That's all I ask."

I went back to sucking her breasts as I slid my fingers inside her again. Her face told me she was digging it. I could feel her legs start to tremble and she was so wet.

"Do you like the feel of my fingers going in and out of your pussy?"

She started to nod her head.

"Kendall," I shouted a bit too loud.

"Yes. I love it," she barely whispered.

"I love it too. Your pussy is so wet and you feel so good. I can't wait to slip my dick inside you."

By now, her eyes were closed again and she was going into that zone. When she started moaning and humming, that was my signal she was almost there.

"Kendall, open your eyes. You wanna feel me deep inside you?"

"Yesss!"

"I know you do."

She wrapped her arms around my back, pulling me closer to her: her signal that she was ready to come.

"Tell me what you want."

"You know."

"Let me hear you say it."

"I wanna feel you inside me."

"Good girl." I smiled.

I stroked her hair, her face. "See, that wasn't so hard. Now we are on the same page."

I positioned myself over her. I was always careful not to put my full weight on her. I am a big man and Kendall is small, petite. She wouldn't be able to handle my full weight pressed against her. Usually, I'd inch inside her, a little at a time, but tonight, I gave her all of me and started pumping away at a steady pace.

"Ahh, damn! Stop, Xavier!"

"Relax, Kendall. Stop fighting it. Just relax," I said, spreading her legs wider with my knees.

I pumped in and out. Up and down. Giving her every inch. Filling her up. I knew she was not used to aggressive sex coming from me. I typically treated her like a princess in the bedroom.

"Ohhhhh!"

"That feels good, doesn't it?"

"Stop! Stop!" she shouted, trying to push me away.

"Kendall, move your hand. You can handle it. Relax, baby."

She moved it away and as soon as I started grinding, she placed it back on my chest.

"Move your hand! Put it on my shoulder or my butt."

"Ohhh, God! Stop!" she shouted, trying to wiggle from underneath me.

I placed my weight on her so she couldn't move. I pinned her down and continued to grind in and out of her at a frantic pace.

"Don't tell me to stop," I whispered into her ear. "I'm your man. If it feels good, why would you want me to stop? Your pussy is wide open."

By now, her face was flushed, she was biting her bottom lip and I knew she was going to come any minute.

"Stop! Don't!" I could tell she was giving up her fight for control. She always wanted to control her orgasm somehow.

I pushed her legs open wider with my knees. I wanted her to feel that she wasn't dealing with a lightweight. If she was going to be my woman, then she had to learn to take it all.

"Didn't I tell you not to tell me to stop? Don't say that shit again," I ordered.

We were staring eye to eye and she knew I was serious.

"Ahhh, you feel so good, girl. You are exactly what the doctor ordered."

I bit down on her neck. Almost there.

"Yesss! Yesss!"

"That's right! Tell me yes! Say yes, I love this dick! Yes, I want this big-ass dick!"

That was all she wrote. She came harder than I had ever seen her come in the past. After her breathing returned to normal, she covered her face with her hands.

"I'm so embarrassed."

"Why? You did good," I said, pulling her hands away from her face, nuzzling her neck.

"Those things I said to you . . ."

"Your words only turned me on more. You have to learn to let loose, Kendall. I like it when you talk dirty to me. Come here."

"What now? Let me rest."

"I haven't forgotten. Get over here and suck this dick," I commanded, holding it up between my fingers.

She looked at me for a moment like she was going to resist, and then she crawled over and positioned herself between my legs.

"Well? What are you waiting for?"

"Tell me what to do."

"Kendall, it's not that hard, damn. Open your mouth and suck. Use a lot of spit and don't bite or scrape your teeth against my dick."

People who knew me said I could be mean as a snake at times. My mom said I got that particular trait from my daddy's side of the family. I didn't know about that, but I knew I was very direct, always had been. Kendall hadn't really seen the mean side of me before. She was a sweet girl; sweet as honey. My anger never had a reason to present itself to her. That was a good thing. After we married, I knew I would have to work with her, to get her to the level of what I expected from a wife. And you best believe, one of the major lessons was to learn how to please me in bed. I was being patient for now because I knew she hadn't had much experience. However, that excuse couldn't last forever.

Kendall gave it the old college try for all of ten minutes. She acted like she was going to choke on my dick; kept gagging. I couldn't complain though. At least she did try, and I wasn't worried because I knew before I was done with her, she'd learn to love it or fake it, one or the other, but she was definitely going to be required to give me head.

As she slept and I held her in my arms, I felt bad that I had been tough on her.

I knew her kitty would be sore the next morning after the pounding I gave her. I think I was a bit pissed at her. As irrational as it was, I think I blamed her for my one night stand with Pilar. The entire time she just simply lay there, waiting for me to do all the damn work, I thought of Pilar and how off the wall the sex was. And, the woman I loved, the woman I should be having spectacular sex with, was just laying here. I figured if Kendall would step up to the plate, I wouldn't have cheated. I could be fulfilled at home.

Totally irrational, I know, but somehow that's how I resolved my feelings of guilt. I fell asleep as visions of Pilar danced across my eyes.

Chapter 9

PILAR

Sex, books, and more sex . . .

I stepped off the glass-enclosed elevator, onto the floor of the ritzy hotel where the three-day conference events were taking place, and I immediately felt the energy of bustling excitement in the air. There were people everywhere. Vendors sold everything from jewelry to perfume to clothing. I observed several book clubs members scampering around showcasing their club colors in everything from caps, T-shirts, bags and buttons.

As I casually walked around, I saw a few faces that looked very familiar. Must be best-selling authors. Avid readers and industry players took photos and acted like it was a literary reunion. Everyone celebrated the common bond of reading and writing in the African-American community. According to what I had been told by organizers of the event, featured authors were holding one-hour discussions in various rooms at assigned times. I had already confirmed interview times with a self-published and mainstream author, including a book club president, agent, editor and publisher. My plate was full for the morning hours.

*   *   *

Three and a half hours later, my work was done. I had enough information to write up an interesting article regarding the state of the African-American literary industry. Now, I was free to hook up with Xavier. According to the schedule I held in my hands, he was featured in exactly thirty minutes in room 203B. Perfect. That gave me exactly enough time to run up to my hotel room, freshen up and change into the pretty floral wraparound dress I purchased especially for this occasion. He had mentioned how he liked bold colors like oranges and yellows. My plan was to walk in toward the end of his presentation and catch him after the groupies had dispersed.

Everything was going perfectly as planned. I walked into the presentation toward the end; according to my watch he had another ten to fifteen minutes, at most, to speak. Xavier had a full house, mostly a female audience. Standing room only. Women loved Xavier Preston . . . and he knew it . . . and he used it to his advantage. When I entered the room, he paused only briefly, but I did see recognition shine in his eyes as we made eye contact. I somehow managed to find an empty chair near the very back of the room and enjoyed the rest of his presentation.

Xavier was an excellent public speaker. He was so down to earth and real that the audience held on to his every word; he was very captivating. I noticed most of the audience had copies of his books in their hands. He answered all the questions that were asked, many of them from aspiring or self-published authors and then he even spent time afterward autographing books, even though they had a scheduled time for that later in the day.

When the last reader was ready to leave, I finally rose from my chair and walked toward the front of the room.

"We meet again."

"Yes, we do. Miss Pilar."

"You remembered?" I smiled.

"Of course. How could I forget you, the woman who made my last trip to Atlanta very memorable? Come here and give me a big hug."

Xavier and I hugged and I simply melted in his strong, firm arms. He smelled wonderful, like the last time.

"So, tell me. What brings you here?" he asked curiously.

"Well, as you may remember, I'm a freelance writer, so I'm covering this event for one of the local magazines."

"Cool."

"It's an added bonus that I ran into you. Just happened to see your name on the schedule."

"You just happened to see my name, huh?"

"Uh-huh."

"By the way, you look very nice," he stated, with his eyes appreciatively roaming across my body. "Those colors look great on you. Complement your complexion."

"Thank you."

"Listen, I have an autograph session in another hour or so, but I'd love to take you to dinner. Have some interesting conversation, catch up and enjoy your company."

"That would be great. I'd like that a lot," I said, smiling because my plan was coming together nicely. This time he would miss me when we parted ways.

Xavier looked down at his watch. "How does eight o'clock sound?"

"Sounds great. I've actually reserved a room here in the hotel, so just come to room 615 when you are ready."

We said our goodbyes until later that night. I headed toward the set of elevators that led upstairs to my room as Xavier was approached by a crowd of adoring fans. Female, of course. They'd better enjoy him now because tonight he was all mine.

Chapter 10

XAVIER

The best of times . . .

Pilar didn't fool me for one minute, not even a second. She just happened to be covering an event where I just happened to be one of the featured authors . . . yeah, right. Do I look like I have stupid stamped on my forehead? I knew she was lying, but I still felt flattered. Flattered that she'd go through so much trouble to seek me out, and it didn't hurt that she was looking drop-dead gorgeous in a dress that was seriously working her curves. Hell, I didn't come to Atlanta that often; if Pilar wanted to hook me up, I wasn't about to turn it down. Like I said, I wasn't stupid.

I walked around, talked to my fans, took pictures, signed copies of my books, passed out flyers, caught up with other authors that all ran in the same circles and around seven o'clock, headed up to my room. By eight-fifteen, Pilar and I were seated at a table in the hotel restaurant, over in the corner. The atmosphere was somewhat romantic, with candles on the tables and dim lighting throughout the restaurant. The tables were spaced far enough apart to ensure an air of privacy and intimacy.

"So, how've you been since the last time I saw you?" I asked, getting comfortable after our waiter brought over my gin and tonic. "What's been going on?"

"Busy. Always working," she said.

"Same here. I always have multiple projects going at one time, but I seem to function best when I'm multi-tasking."

"Do you attend these types of events all the time?" Pilar questioned.

"Yeah, pretty much. I go wherever I'm requested. The book business is all about sales, and to obtain sales you have to have exposure. If some organization pays for my travel and expenses and I have the opportunity to promote and talk about my books, then I'm there. Book clubs, festivals, conferences, colleges and universities, I do them all."

"Wow! That sounds exciting," Pilar said, leaning back in her chair. "I can tell you truly love what you do."

"Actually, it gets pretty boring after a while. Once you've seen one of these events you've seen them all. But you are right, I do love writing; it's in my blood. At home, I work hard, and play even harder on the road."

"Do you now?" she asked seductively.

"I sure do. You should know."

"How should I know?" she asked.

"You're here, aren't you? You came back for more." I leaned back in my chair and silently dared her to deny it.

"Whatever."

"You know you're whipped," I leaned over the table and whispered. "Admit it."

"I don't know. Tell me. What does whipped feel like?" she inquired.

I played along. "When you saw me earlier today, did you get wet thinking about the things I did to you last time we were together?"

"Yes," she giggled, after pausing to think about it.

"Have you thought about me sexing you since we've been apart?"

"Yes. All the time," she whispered, with her eyes never breaking their hold with mine.

"Sounds like you're whipped to me." I laughed.

"And what if I am? Is that a bad thing?"

"No, not at all."

Pilar took a long sip of her white wine. She really didn't eat a lot because she had barely touched her fried catfish and mixed vegetables. Me, I was working on my second gin and tonic and my entrée of steak and potatoes was almost finished.

"Tell me about yourself, Pilar."

She shrugged her shoulders, not interested. "There's not much to tell. My life is not nearly as exciting as yours. I'm a journalist who has the luxury of working freelance due to inheritances I received a few years ago."

"You are a trust fund baby?"

"I guess you can say that. I came into some money due to death."

"I wish one of my distant relatives would die and leave me a shitload of cash," I kidded.

"It was my mother and stepfather."

"Oh, Pilar. I'm sorry, I didn't mean to . . ."

"No, it's okay. It is what it is," she stated very matter-of-factly. "We all have to go sometime. When it's your time, it's your time."

I thought that was odd, to talk about your parents with no emotion. This chick ran on hot and cold.

"Wow! I never really knew my father, but I couldn't imagine my mom not being in my life."

"You'd be surprised at what you can handle when you have to."

I looked at her strangely. "I guess so."

"I know so."

She took another bite of fish and slowly chewed, like she was counting the number of chews before she swallowed.

"Are you originally from Atlanta, Pilar?"

"No, I moved here a few years ago from Baltimore."

"Baltimore. The women love me out there, too" I said, attempting to make the mood somewhat lighter.

She laughed. Pilar had a terrific laugh. Like it just erupted out of her, somewhere deep within and only came out for special occasions. I observed that most of the time she seemed to be analyzing the moment. Almost studying me.

"You know what? You are so arrogant. So full of yourself," she said out of the clear blue. "You are dangerous."

"No, not arrogant, baby, just sure of myself. There's a difference."

"I like when you call me baby."

That statement kind of threw me off guard, so I didn't comment one way or the other. I couldn't tell if she was serious or not.

"What do you do when you aren't writing? A beautiful woman such as yourself, I'm sure the men are knocking down your door."

"Not really. I'm very particular about who I give myself to."

She could have fooled me.

"I know what you're thinking, but really I am. Before I was with you, I hadn't slept with a man in over a year, and I haven't slept with anyone since I last saw you."

"Damn, girl!"

"What? Do you find that odd? Hard to believe?"

"No. Whatever floats your boat. Couldn't be me though."

She shook her head and giggled.

"What?"

"You are funny. You make me laugh."

"No, just direct. I speak my mind. No holds barred with me. Take me or leave me, baby, but I'm going to bring it to you straight, with no chaser."

"I like it, your directness. I like you, too."

I took a huge swallow of my drink and looked around the crowded restaurant. When I looked back, she was still staring at me.

"Oh, you are just going to leave me hanging?"

"What do you mean?" I asked.

"Oh, now you're trying to play dumb. I told you I like you and you didn't respond. Do you like me?"

"You sound like a sixth grader, straight out of elementary school. I don't even know you and you don't know me. This is what it is. Do you want me to put a name on it?" I said, leaning back in my chair. I dared her to ask me to name it.

For a second, I saw this look cross her face, like, *who the fuck do you think you talking to*, and then it vanished just as quickly. In a flash. If I had blinked, I would have missed it.

"I don't know you? So, tell me. Tell me about yourself. What's your story?" she said.

"Five words. I'm a self-made man. Everything I have, I got it on my own. From my own sweat and blood. I've never had anything handed to me on a silver platter. I've worked hard for every cent I've ever earned."

Pilar nodded, silently prompting me to go on.

"At one point, my life was going in the wrong direction, but I chose to turn that around. Put all that thugged-out shit behind me. People in my neighborhood had pretty much written me off anyway; thought I'd end up being another statistic or lying in an early grave. I proved them all wrong. Every last one of them. Now, I'm crafting stories and paying the bills. Keeping my lights on."

"That is truly amazing. Such an inspiring success story."

"What you see is what you get. I'm probably one of the realest brothers you will ever meet."

"Really now?"

"That's what I said," I responded back.

"Looks can be deceiving."

"Not always. I have your number," I said.

"And what's my number, Xavier?" she asked smoothly.

"You are a woman who knows exactly what she wants and goes after it."

"Hmmm. A quote from one of my favorite authors, Maya Angelou: 'when people show you who they are, believe them.'"

"I know what I see," I said, taking another gulp of my drink.

"Is that good or bad?" she asked.

"For me, it's good. I don't care for bullshit games."

"Good. We are on the same page then. Won't be any hurt feelings."

"True." I thought to myself that this was a bold and aggressive woman.

"I bet you have a woman back in Houston who doesn't have a clue, not a clue, what you're doing in Atlanta."

"You think so?" I asked.

"No, I pretty much know so."

"Enlighten me then, Miss Pilar."

"Men like you always have some woman waiting in the wings, head over heels in love with you. Would do almost anything for you. Until they get fed up with your shit."

"Are you finished?"

"Not quite. Men like you can never get over the desire for new pussy. Always searching, always on the hunt. Am I right?"

"You tell me. You got me all figured out, men like me."

"I know you have a woman back in Houston."

"And if I do, would it matter to you, Pilar?"

"No," she said without stuttering or blinking an eye. "Your woman is not my concern. That's between you and her."

"That's what I thought. So, there's nothing more to discuss, is there?" I questioned, not breaking eye contact.

"I guess not. You're grown, I'm grown," she said and smiled sweetly. "We are two consenting adults. And I love what you do to me with that big-ass dick."

"At this moment in time, I'm here with you. Enjoying interesting conversation, a fine meal and an even finer woman."

I lifted my glass for a toast. Pilar lifted hers in turn and clicked it against mine.

"Let's just enjoy the moment," I requested.

She nodded in agreement.

"Tonight's our night."

"I have just one more question for you."

"Go ahead, ask it. I'm going to let you ask all your questions and get them out of your system, Miss Pilar."

"Did you miss me sucking your dick?"

Damn, this chick was bold.

"What do you think?"

"I don't think. I know you did," Pilar stated seductively, leaning in toward me. "I bet you money that when you were back in Houston, screwing your woman, you had flashbacks of me going down on you."

"Now, let me ask you a question."

"I'm listening," she said.

"Do you think about sex twenty-four-seven? Because you are one of the few women I've met who doesn't play games when it comes to her sexuality."

"Not twenty-four-seven, but I do think about ways to please you throughout the day."

"You are too much, Pilar. Your man has his hands full with you."

"I told you before I don't have a man. Not yet anyway. I'm looking, and I may have found someone."

"Well, when you find him, he is going to have his hands full with you. Will have to tame your ass."

"Oh, no you didn't! What century are you living in, Xavier?"

I laughed. "I'm just messing with you. I love a feisty woman; you are all right with me. But seriously, let's just make a deal to enjoy tonight."

"Deal." She reached her hand across the table and we literally shook on it.

For the rest of the night, that is exactly what we did . . . enjoyed the night. After we made our way back upstairs to my room, Pilar gave herself to me in unimaginable ways. She couldn't get enough. I had to stop after we went through an entire box of condoms.

Pilar was insatiable. She did things and let me do things to her that Kendall would never allow. Not even in another lifetime. Even though I had decided that this was the last fling I was going to have with any of these scandalous females I met on the road, I couldn't help thinking that I wished Kendall had an ounce of what Pilar had sexually.

At the crack of dawn, Pilar and I finally sought sleep as the sun slowly rose over the city, announcing another day in the Peach State. Tangled in each other's arms, I don't think either of us moved until close to noon. Didn't have the energy to. Personally, I felt like Pilar had drained every ounce of fluid out of me. And she swallowed.

After rising and taking a quick shower, I had to make a mad dash for the airport. I don't know why the alarm clock never went off; I had set it the night before, even double-checked it. I wanted to make sure I awoke in plenty of time to make my flight home. I left Pilar in my hotel room, still buck naked under the sheets, smelling like sex. She looked so sad to see me leave, like she was about to cry. This chick confused me at times.

As I gave her a goodbye kiss, the last thing she said caused me to pause, but I didn't have time to confront her.

"Have a safe trip home, babe. I'll talk to you soon."

Chapter 11

PILAR

Sunshine on my shoulders makes me happy . . .

I was on a natural high, a Xavier high; didn't need to take any medication to make me feel better. I had Xavier Preston's private phone number. When he went into the bathroom to shower, he thought I was fast asleep. I wasn't. I could play possum with the best of them. I used Xavier's time in the shower to dial my cell phone number from his phone. When my phone silently vibrated, I captured his number. I quickly deleted any evidence from his phone. Pretty smart, huh?

While I was doing this, he received a text message from some chick named Kendall. I quickly deleted it and made a note of the name and phone number. After last night, Xavier wouldn't have a need for any other woman in his life. I could provide anything he needed; mentally, emotionally and definitely sexually. After last night, he definitely knew I could provide sexually.

Yesterday confirmed my belief that Xavier and I were meant for each other. Sexually, we meshed together like peanut butter and jelly, ketchup and mustard, ham and cheese. From the conversation at dinner, I realized his life hadn't been peaches and cream either, and I knew for a fact mine hadn't. He succeeded in spite of everything. We were two peas in a pod. We complemented each other in ways beyond my wildest imagination. When Xavier simply looked at me, my heart went pitter-patter. I had finally found the one I had been waiting for. My wait was over. Soon he'd realize it, too.

Before I left his hotel room and checked out of mine, I had the next stage of my plan already outlined in my head. This man was going to love me even if it killed him. Like the famous song from *Dreamgirls*, he was going to love me. There was no way I was living without him.

I hadn't yet made it to Interstate 85 before I began texting. I was happy there wasn't much traffic on the downtown streets because I wouldn't want to cause an accident.

Hey babe, did you make your plane?

I waited a few seconds for Xavier to text back. I didn't realize I was holding my breath until he answered and I exhaled.

Yeah. I have fifteen minutes before I board.

I was still pissed that my plan for him to miss his plane hadn't worked. Yeah, I turned off the alarm the night before. I figured if he missed his plane, I could talk him into staying an extra night. An additional night with me.

Did you have fun last night?

The best. This had me beaming.

I wrote, **I miss you already and I really like you. You are good people.**

Minutes passed and I kept looking from the road to my BlackBerry. I almost swayed into another lane and sideswiped a car. I was getting more and more anxious by the second. Finally, Xavier texted back.

Take care, Pilar. I am boarding, gotta run. Be good.

Bye. Talk soon, I swiftly typed back. My eyes teared up a bit. At least when he was in Georgia, Xavier and I were in the same state, breathing the same air. Texas seemed so far away, like another country.

I glanced into my rearview mirror and carefully pulled over to the side of the road to retrieve the slip of paper from my purse, carefully hidden at the bottom. The paper from the hotel that I had written the name and phone number on. I retrieved my second BlackBerry from the dashboard and turned it on. This number was registered under a fake name.

Taking my time, savoring the moment, I typed in Kendall's phone number, then wrote: **I enjoyed sucking your man's dick this weekend. He came all in my mouth. Hmm, hmm, good.**

Chapter 12

XAVIER

Today was a good day . . . not!

All was quiet in my world. Peace and tranquility. Just the way I liked it. Believe it or not, I'm a very traditional type of guy. Some might even call me conservative when it comes to relationships. I like for my home life to be drama free and a haven for myself. When it comes down to it, I'm a very simple, down to earth man. After Pilar went ballistic texting me at the airport, sending one text message after another, I just knew I'd probably have to tell her off, in a nice way, if she started that shit again when I arrived home.

Over the years I've developed a three-step rule to deter unwanted female attention via the Internet: 1) I limit my e-mail responses to one or two words. 2) I politely tell the person she is e-mailing me excessively. 3) I curse the psycho bitch out and tell her in no uncertain terms not to contact me again.

It appeared I wouldn't have to use drastic measures with Pilar because all was serene. Out of sight, out of mind. Even Kendall was quiet. I hadn't seen her since I returned, but had only talked with her briefly. She explained she was super busy with school. That was cool because I was proud of my baby and wanted her to do her best: to be the best. I didn't want to be a distraction. Plus, our separation gave me more time to write.

Unfortunately, I spoke a little too soon. By the end of the week, I received an e-mail in the middle of my morning writing schedule. I heard the all too familiar *you've got mail.*

I clicked to read, Hey, babe. I haven't heard from you. What's up?

I didn't respond. I kept right on typing, working on the first draft of my manuscript.

I know you are online because we both use AOL and you are my only buddy. I see you online.

I still didn't comment.

Answer me, babe. Are you busy?

I quickly typed off an e-mail before I lost my creative flow.

Pilar, I'm in the middle of my morning writing routine. I can't talk right now. Chatting ruins my flow.

You don't even have a minute to say hello? I haven't talked to you in five long days. Damn, babe. Are you serious?

I didn't answer. Tried my best to ignore her.

Take a small break, please. Please, babe?

Okay, I will this one time, but you can't continue to interrupt me with these e-mails, Pilar. Damn!

Okay, I won't interrupt. It will not happen again. I promise. Are you happy now?

Good because I don't like e-mailing. I don't do e-mails. Period.

So . . . do you miss me yet?

No! Damn, she irritated the hell out of me with that question.

No? You know what, you are mean! You don't care about my feelings.

I'm being honest. I don't know you well enough to miss you.

What about last Saturday?

What about it? We fucked.

Why are you being so mean to me? Saying these hurtful things. Intentionally trying to hurt my feelings.

I'm not, Pilar. I'm simply telling you the truth, but you don't want the truth. You can't handle that. You want to hear some convoluted bullshit version you've dreamed up in that pretty head of yours.

So, you are saying you haven't thought about me one time?

No. Not one time.

I don't believe you.

That's your prerogative. Believe what you wish.

You don't miss me?

Nope. Not at all. This chick was unbelievable. Relentless.

I thought we connected at dinner. I know we connected in bed. I thought you were feeling me and vice versa. I thought we were on the same page.

Keep your emotions out of the equation.

But I thought . . .

Pilar, are you delusional? I don't want to hurt your feelings because I think you are a very nice woman, but the only connection we have is that we both like to fuck . . . each other. You have a strong sexual appetite and so do I.

But I was feeling you . . .

I repeat, keep your emotions out of the equation . . .

YOU KNOW WHAT? I HATE YOUR ASS SO MUCH RIGHT NOW! she screamed at me by using all caps.

I typed quickly. I'm not exactly liking your ass right now either.

Remember what I told you at dinner? When people show you who they are, believe them. Well, I'm *telling* you now. DON'T FUCK WITH ME, XAVIER!

**Get a life, bitch. Your pussy wasn't that damn good.
I've had better.**

FUCK YOU, XAVIER!

I stood up and pulled away from my computer, mad as hell, knocking my chair to the floor. What was up with this chick? Hell no, I didn't miss her crazy ass. Blowing up my damn e-mail like it was going out of style. I'm glad I made the decision before I left Georgia to quit fucking around. Maybe that's why this crazy-ass Georgia bitch crossed my path, so that I could get the message loud and clear. Damn! I was so angry I couldn't even write anymore, couldn't concentrate. Had to go downstairs and work out, work off some of my tension and stress by lifting weights.

Two hours later, I was feeling a little better. I always felt refreshed after I exercised, but my day was still wasted; I wasn't good for anything. I decided to give myself a free day and start back writing tomorrow. With time on my hands, I decided to call my baby. Little did I know she'd have a stick up her ass, too.

"Hey, baby!"

"Who is this?"

"What do you mean who is this?" I asked, my voice rising by an octave. "You'd better know my voice by now."

"Oh, hey, Xavier," she said with major attitude.

"Is that all the love I get today?" I asked.

"Didn't you get enough in Atlanta?" she asked coldly, out of the blue.

For a second, my blood ran cold. Chills ran up and down my arms.

"What did you say?"

"You heard me. Didn't you get enough in Atlanta?"

"I don't know what you're talking about. I don't need this today. Yeah, I got a lot of love from the book club members who came out to support me by purchasing my books and spreading the word."

"What about from the woman who sucked your dick?" she yelled.

For a minute, I was speechless. I couldn't believe my baby was so mad that she screamed at me and repeated vulgarities. Kendall just wasn't the type, and that was what immediately attracted me to her. She was refined, quiet and understated.

"Excuse me?"

"Xavier, how could you do this to me? To us?" Next all I heard were loud, uncontrollable sobs.

"Baby, please don't cry. You know I can't stand to hear you cry. Calm down and tell me what's going on. You know I'd never hurt you because I love you too much. So what are you talking about?"

"Last Sunday, I received a text message from someone claiming you had been with her in Atlanta."

"You are just telling me about this? What else did it say?"

"That was all except for the fact that you loved her oral skills."

"And you honestly believed it?"

Silence.

"Huh, I guess you did. Don't you know by now that you are the only woman for me?"

"I thought I was. I'm not so sure now."

"You are, baby. I've explained what it's like being a celebrity author. Women act crazy sometimes. Do and say crazy shit."

"How did this person get my cell number?" she asked.

"Hell, I don't know. Who are you asking? People will find whatever they want to find. You can get anything over the Internet. Do you really think if I was with another woman, I'd give her your cell number?"

More silence.

"Think about how crazy this all sounds," I asked as convincingly as possible.

She hesitated for a few seconds. "True."

"You saw the schedule before I left. I had full days of activities. I barely had any downtime. When I went to bed at night,

I crashed and was out for the count. There was no woman in my bed."

The crying had subsided somewhat. I still heard a few sniffles here and there like she was trying to compose herself.

"Xavier, promise me the text message was a lie. I couldn't stand for you to hurt me, and I don't understand why someone would be so malicious."

"I promise, baby. I love you, Kendall. I'd never hurt you."

"I love you so much and I couldn't take you betraying me like that," she said. "You know the trust issues I have because of my last boyfriend."

With that off her chest, Kendall appeared to relax and we made plans to see each other the next day. We hung up on good terms again. I don't know how Pilar got Kendall's cell number, but I saw now that she was not one to play with. I had underestimated her.

Chapter 13

PILAR

There's nothing like a woman scorned.

After I had completely destroyed my bedroom in a mad, un-relentless rage, I was now sprawled on the floor, trying to catch my breath as snot and tears ran down my face in steady streams. My bed linens were in a cluttered pile on the floor, over near my dresser. All the knickknacks that sat on top of it were now on the floor beneath. My ceramic lamp had been shattered and tossed to the floor, sharp pieces all over the place. Framed pictures were knocked off the wall and clothes strewn everywhere, pulled haphazardly out of drawers. I totally trashed my room in an uncontrollable outrage and destroyed everything in my path.

I paced back and forth, from one wall of my bedroom to the other, mumbling to myself. I pounded my fist against my fore-head.

How dare he say those things to me? How dare he? I'll show that motherfucker not to mess with me. I'll show him. I'll make him pay. Men are all the same. They want one thing: what's between a woman's legs. Once they get that, they are gone. Gone! Gone! Gone! Poof!

I gave him everything. I told him things about myself that I didn't have to share. I did all that sick, perverted sexual stuff he wanted me to do. Why? Why? Because I wanted to please him. Did he care that I was uncomfortable doing it? Did he even notice? Hell, no!

It's always about what they want. What pleases them. Self-serving, self-absorbed bastards. Think about me for once. One time. Think about my needs, my desires. No one ever thinks about me.

Psycho bitch? I'll show him who's a psycho bitch. He wasn't calling me a psycho bitch when he was eating me out or pounding my pussy. I hate, absolutely hate his black ass. Don't treat me like a piece of fucking meat and think I don't have any feelings. Keep my emotions to myself? How am I supposed to not catch any feelings? Keep my emotions to myself? I'm not a cold, heartless piece of shit like him. I feel. Ask the others. Ask them what happens when you treat me like nothing.

See, now he has me bringing up old memories, bad memories. Memories I left behind in Baltimore. I'll show him a "psycho bitch." When I get through with him he'll be sorry he ever said those nasty, mean things to me. He'll be extra sorry he ever met me. He'll regret the day he opened his mouth to speak to me.

I give, give, give of myself and this is what I receive in return. Nothing, absolutely nothing. And his precious girlfriend, Kendall. What's so special about her? What is she doing for him that's so special? Not much, evidently. He is coming to me to get his sexual needs fulfilled. Fucking me. Banging me. Screwing me. So, what is she doing for you! What has she done for you lately? Answer that. I bet she doesn't let you come in her mouth. I bet she's a prude who doesn't even enjoy sex. Simply lies there and lets you handle your business.

Talking to me like I ain't nothing. I'll show you. Just wait. I'll show you. I'll show your ass. You mean motherfucker. You'll eat those words, choke them out. Just wait and see.

Just because you are a published author, that don't mean shit to me. Acting like you all that and then some. Acting all special. Like your shit don't stink. You weren't acting like you were all that when you had your thumb stuck up my ass, licking my clit. Your dick wasn't all that either. Your skills aren't all that you think they are. Maybe you're the delusional one. I've had better dick, too. Much better. Three times better!

I hate you. I absolutely hate you. I hate you Xavier Preston! Can you hear me in Texas? I hate you! You mean nothing to me. Absolutely nothing. If you were here, I'd spit in your face. I've met men like you my entire life, men who think the sun rises and sets around them. Not! In the grand scheme of things . . . you are simply not that important. Get over yourself!

For the next hour I sobbed my eyes out, curled up in the fetal position on the floor next to my bed. By the time my sobbing subsided, my eyes were so red and swollen I could barely see. When I finally got the strength to get off the floor, I went to the kitchen and prepared a single slice of cinnamon toast and drank some hot tea. My comfort foods. My aunt used to make those for me when I was sick as a child. Now, when I didn't feel well, I made them for myself.

By the time I finished my snack, I was starting to feel like my old self again. All was good. Even soul mates have disagreements. That's life. People aren't perfect. We make mistakes and we forgive. Maybe not forget, but we forgive and move on.

I quickly went to my laptop and typed the following e-mail:

Babe, I forgive you. I know you didn't mean those mean things you said. I realize you were simply having a bad day and chose to take it out on me. I understand. Really, I do. I'm here for you. I miss you so much and I know you miss me. Hugs and kisses, Pilar.

Chapter 14

XAVIER

Why do I feel like I'm in the Twilight Zone?
"Demented, crazy-ass bitch!" Damn, she had me riled up again! I have never had a woman get under my skin like Pilar did. All I could do was shake my head when I received another e-mail from her. Was she on another planet or what? I started to confront her about the text message my baby received, but I couldn't prove anything. I'm sure she would deny, deny, deny anyway. Plus, I didn't want another confrontation with Pilar. I simply wanted her to leave me the hell alone. She was in Georgia and I was in Texas, thank goodness for the 800 miles that separated us. Thank God. Pressing delete on her e-mail brought me great joy.

Pilar had me so out of sorts that I was acting totally out of character, throwing my routine totally off. I picked up the phone and dialed one of my partners at his J-O-B. Dré was as close to me as a brother and was one of the few people I still hung with from back in the day. He was a lot like me; wanted to make something of his life, which he had. He was doing well as vice president of a local bank and was always giving back by way of his time and money to our old neighborhood.

He regularly spoke to at risk boys at various venues and tried to show them there was another way besides drugs and violence.

"Hey, what's up, my nigga?"

"Hey, man, don't be calling my job talking that ghetto slang." He laughed. "Hold on, let me close my office door so I can talk like I want to. Be real for a minute."

There was a short pause.

"Okay, I'm back. What's up, dog?" he screamed.

"Not much."

"Wait a minute, hold up. In all the years I've been here, I don't think you have ever called me at work. What's going on?" he asked.

"Can't a man call up his best friend?" I questioned, beating around the bush.

"Man, who do you think you're talking to? This is Dré. I know you like I know my damn self. You don't roll like that. You don't even like talking on the damn phone."

"Things change."

"Yeah, right. Since when? When I called you during your *writing time* last week, you went off on me for at least ten minutes, bit my head off about interrupting your so called flow before I could even tell you I had two tickets for the game."

"You're right."

"I know I am. What's on your mind, my brother? Didn't you just return from Atlanta?"

"Yeah."

"I haven't been to the ATL in a while. I still remember those fine-ass women, though, but they were too high maintenance for my blood."

"They are still there, haven't gone anywhere, still looking good." I laughed. I could almost picture Dré drooling all over himself at just the visual image alone.

"Now that you are the big-time celebrity author, it doesn't matter what city you are in; these women jock your dick like crazy, man. I've seen it up close and personal."

"What can I say?" I declared, playfully popping my collar.

"Say you will send some of those groupies my way."

"Man, you don't want my sloppy seconds."

"We can do it like we used to back in the day. Remember those twins, that cheap-ass motel and the two bottles of Boones Farm wine?"

I laughed. "We have come a long way."

"That we have," Dré agreed. "That we have."

"Have you closed any big deals lately?"

"Come on, man. What's really going on? You know you don't care about me landing any deals the same as I don't care about some romance novel you're working on."

"Okay, you got me. Here's the skinny. Short version, I met this hot chick in Atlanta and we hooked up."

"Doesn't sound like a problem to me, but I thought you had let all that go."

"I did. I had. But this chick, she's different. There is just something about her. She has this needy, vulnerable side that she tries hard to keep under wraps, yet she is like a tiger defending her cubs in the bedroom. Very aggressive. She'd literally do anything I asked her to."

"Wow. Hooked you up, huh?"

"You best believe it. It was very hard to walk away from that piece."

"Be careful. Kendall is a sweet girl, and she must be special if she got you to pop the question. I still can't believe my man is engaged to be married and I'm the best man. You wouldn't want to lose her because you couldn't keep your dick in your pants."

"You are preaching to the choir, and that's what I'm afraid of. I'm scared to death of losing her."

"I don't understand. You've lost me now. You tapped that ass with the ATL chick, had fun and walked away. Kendall doesn't know. And best believe, what she doesn't know won't hurt her."

"I wish it were that simple. This Pilar chick . . . now she won't leave me alone."

"What do you mean she won't leave you alone?"

"Just what I said. She keeps e-mailing me and I think she sent a text to Kendall, telling her how we kicked it."

"Damn! How'd she get your woman's phone number?"

"Who knows? She's a freelance writer; maybe she has connections. Bottom line, she got it."

"Damn! You always manage to get yourself into situations, always over some tail. Remember that time you were messing with that chick from New Orleans and you thought she had put some roots on you?" Dré asked and immediately burst into laughter.

"Man, I'm serious and you're trying to be a comedian." I was trying hard not to chuckle myself. "That shit was not funny." I could look back on it now and laugh, since it was in the past.

"I'm sorry, but that shit *was* funny as hell. You went back down there, to New Orleans, trying to find somebody who could take it off. Looking for a Voodoo Priestess. Said you found a handmade doll under your bed, made out of rags, with pins sticking out of it and your dirty drawers buried in the back yard. Hilarious as hell. When you met her, when you and I were at that restaurant, I told you she was going to be trouble."

"Let me let you get back to work since you are getting laughs at my expense," I said, getting ready to hang up. "Don't quit your day job."

"Hold up, man. Don't get all bent out of shape. Damn! Let me get serious, but this particular situation is simple."

"Okay, that's more like it."

"I'm just appreciating this moment. Xavier Preston calling me for advice. I've got to mark this date on my calendar."

"I know. Am I crazy?" I laughed. "The world must be coming to an end real soon if I'm asking you for advice."

"Seriously, man. It's simple. Don't respond to her e-mails. Cease all contact with her. Deny, deny, deny to your future wifey. And whatever you do, no matter how good the pussy is, don't take any return trips to the cookie jar. Keep your ass and your dick out of Georgia."

"Man, it was good. I'm not even going to lie. She'd get all soppy wet; I'd stick my fingers inside her and pull them out dripping with her juices. I couldn't wait to get all up in that. And she'd spread her legs, open them wide for daddy, and I'd ease up in it real slow."

"Well, forget all that now. You might as well get her out of your system. Ain't no going back to the well. Ever. The well has run dry."

"You're right. Absolutely right," I said.

"I know I am."

"I feel better already. I knew all this, but this chick got me so wound up that I had to hear it from someone I trust because I'm not thinking rationally right now."

"Well, you're straight now, and I might clown on you about our past adventures, but I always got your back, man."

"Yours too."

"Let me get off this phone. Some of us don't have the luxury of working from home. I have deals to close and money to make."

"Okay, I have to bounce, too. Peace."

"Peace."

Little did I know I'd be wishing for peace in the weeks and months to follow. Peace and tranquility no longer resided in my home. Hurricane Psycho Bitch was about to blow through. She was most definitely a Category 5.

Chapter 15

PILAR

I'm ready for love.

I was taking an afternoon break from finishing up an article on *How to Find Anything About Anybody on the Internet* when I decided I would give Leeda a call.

"How've you been?" Leeda asked.

"Okay I guess."

"Where is all that excitement from a few weeks ago?"

"It's still here," I said, with not an ounce of enthusiasm in my tone.

"It doesn't sound like it. What's wrong?"

"If you must know, Xavier and I had an argument. Our very first."

"An argument?"

"Yes. We aren't really speaking right now. I'm giving him time to calm down and forgive me. Which I know he will."

"Wait. Slow down. I realize you and I didn't talk last week, but have I missed something?" Leeda asked.

"Not really."

"Sounds like I've missed a lot. You need to catch me up."

"Well, I ran into Xavier at this literary conference a couple of weeks ago."

"Why didn't you tell me the last time we talked?"

"I don't know. Sometimes, I want to have my private moments, just for myself."

"You just happened to run into him, of all people," she inquired.

"Leeda, my God, it was a literary event I was covering! Of course there was the possibility he would be attending in a major market like Atlanta."

"I guess so."

"It wasn't like I planned it. Fate has a way of stepping in sometimes. Anyway, I saw him there and we ended up fucking in his hotel room."

"Why do you always refer to a natural, loving act in such crude, unrefined terms?"

"Men don't know how to make love. They fuck. That's what Xavier did to me; he fucked me, Leeda, and he did it very well. He claims I'm whipped and he may be right. I absolutely live to feel him inside me, expanding. He makes my body come alive and he feels so good."

"You are giving me way too much detail, Pilar."

"Well, it's true. He has the biggest, thickest, prettiest dick I've ever seen and he's all man. A real man."

"A real man?"

"Yes. You know I'm attracted to men who are aggressive, direct and protective of their woman, yet can put her in her place. A real man wears the pants in the relationship and his woman wants to cater to him because he treats her right. He comes correct. That's Xavier."

"You mentioned he was mad at you. Why is he mad at you?" Leeda asked.

"Oh, just something stupid I did."

"What?"

"Xavier claims, notice I say *claims*, I was e-mailing him excessively. Can you believe that?"

"Are you? Were you?"

"No! I don't think so. A few e-mails a day is not excessive. I don't care what he says. He thinks I'm supposed to abide by his rules like he can tell me what to do, like I'm supposed to accommodate his every request. He's not the boss of me."

"Well, just respect the man's wishes."

"If I did, I wouldn't have any contact at all with him. It's not like I talk on the phone with him."

"Would that be a bad thing if you didn't have any more contact with this man? Would you really want to establish a long-term relationship with such a womanizing man?"

"Oh, here we go again," I said with annoyance in my tone.

"What?" Leeda asked like she didn't have a clue what I was talking about.

"Xavier is not using me. I want everything he gives me and then some. Don't you understand, I can't get enough of this man? I crave him like I need air. I'd be with him twenty-four-seven if I could."

"I think you are reading much more into this casual affair than is really there. He doesn't even want you to e-mail him. Think about it. That speaks volumes."

"I think he could love me, if . . ." I caught myself in time. Leeda could be so judgmental. Like her shit never stank.

"If what?" she asked.

"Nothing. It doesn't matter."

"Yes, it does. Tell me."

"If his girlfriend wasn't in the picture."

"He has a girlfriend? See, this proves he is simply using you as a booty call when he's in Atlanta."

"No, it proves that if she were out of the way, he could love me. We wouldn't have to sneak around."

"Well, she isn't out of the way."

"I'm working on it."

"What did you do? Tell me you didn't do anything," Leeda asked with alarm in her voice.

"I texted her and informed her I had been screwing her man."

"Pilar!"

"All's fair in love and war. I'm playing to win and taking no prisoners."

"Pilar, please don't get hurt. I think you are reading more into this *relationship* than there is."

"Oh, Leeda. You are such a worrywart. I'm a big girl and I know how to hang with the big boys. Xavier would never hurt me. He's a little mad with me right now, said some mean things to me, but we'll get past this once he calms down. I know we will."

I had done my research. The Internet was just a wealth of information if you knew where to look. I now knew where Xavier lived, had his exclusive address. I had a map that took me straight to his front door. Even had his home phone number. As for his little precious, soon-to-be ex-girlfriend, I had info on her ass, too. Yeah, I had done my homework. I didn't half step. One thing about being a journalist, you pick up great research skills. I could find anybody and their third cousin once removed if I wanted to.

After hanging up with Leeda, I decided to take a quick nap. Sometimes, she drained me with her fifty questions. Sometimes, I think she lived vicariously through me.

My dreams were filled with visions of Xavier. Xavier's dimples. Xavier's smile. Xavier's huge hands. Xavier's hands as they roamed across my body like he owned it. Xavier doing unimaginable things to me as he whispered seductive words in my ear. Xavier, Xavier, Xavier. I couldn't wait to see my soul mate again.

I wished I could see his face when he received the package that I had sent to him via his agent a couple of days ago. I overnighted it. The last image I had before I drifted off into a deep, dream-filled sleep was an image of a nude Xavier climbing into bed with me by his side.

When I woke up around six o'clock, the first thing I did was to send an e-mail: Hey, babe. I hope your evening is going well. I miss you, Pilar.

As an afterthought, I sent off another.

Babe, send me a photo of your dick; I've almost forgotten what it looks like. I just remember it's huge (smile).

Finally, I sent the last e-mail of the evening.

I wish you would find it in your heart to forgive me. I sincerely didn't mean to offend you, disrespect you or for you to take my words out of context. Please forgive me. I hate the thought of you being mad at me. I *need* to talk to you. Pilar. P.S. Sleep tight, don't let the bed bugs bite.

For the last few days, I had sent Xavier two, three, four, five e-mails daily. I e-mailed him my thoughts, observations. He never responded back. He basically ignored me, but I knew he would come around. I could feel it; it was just a matter of time. I had all the time in the world. He was going to love me even if it killed him because there was no way I was living without him.

Chapter 16

XAVIER

*W*ater under the bridge . . .

When my agent called, left a voice message stating he was going to fax some articles over that he thought I'd find interesting, I didn't know what to think. I turned on my fax machine and twenty minutes later, I was reading three different, very well written articles that had been penned all about me.

The first one focused on my rise from the ghetto to superstar writer status. The second focused on my new book release and how female readers would love it because I had the uncanny ability to delve into the mind of the female psyche, and the third and final article focused on my attendance and participation at the National Book Club Festival. It talked about how I captivated the audience with my presentation. All three articles had the one-name byline, Pilar.

According to the note from my agent, Douglas, he had received an overnight package with the articles enclosed; Pilar asked that he forward them to me. A sticky note he found inside the package stated the articles would appear in *Upscale* magazine, *Today's Black Woman* and *Essence* in the following months. Douglas suggested I personally thank whoever this

Pilar person was because she had given me tons of free publicity, which translated into sales, which translated into money in my bank account.

Throughout the day, I thought that maybe I had misjudged her. Maybe I jumped to conclusions. Pilar didn't have to write those articles, especially after the horrible things I said to her. By no means was Pilar free of fault either; she said some pretty foul things to me as well, but she certainly didn't have to submit her articles for publication after that exchange. A lesser person would have said fuck him and kept it moving.

By lunchtime, before I fixed a quick sandwich, I realized it wouldn't hurt to send Pilar a thank you note via e-mail. I had learned to never burn any bridges. I swiftly penned an e-mail and sent it before I changed my mind.

> Hey, you. Listen, let's squash our differences and move on. Life is too short and I don't want you to think badly of me. My agent sent the articles you wrote. You certainty didn't have to do that, but thank you. I appreciate it. You made my life, my writings, me as a person sound so intriguing. It's obvious you put a lot of research, hard work and passion into the articles. Regardless of what I said previously, you are good people. Thank you and take care, Xavier.

As soon as I hit the button to send it on its way, I instantly felt a cold chill and Dré's words came back to haunt me. I could only pray they didn't come back and bite me. It was too late now. It was on its way to Pilar. Hopefully, the fallout would be positive.

By late evening, I was pleasantly surprised that I hadn't received any e-mail from Pilar. I couldn't believe it. I just knew she was going to blow up my e-mail, but she didn't. Didn't even e-mail me once. Maybe she had taken my small gesture as a peace offering and had finally moved on.

Weeks passed and then a month. Before I knew it, it was late September. Fall was in the air. My life slowly returned to normal. My writing was back on track, deadlines and all. Kendall and I were getting along great. My life was peaceful and serene: no drama—just as I liked it. My agent even spoke of a possible movie deal. Yes. Life was good. I loved my life.

If anyone had asked me about Pilar, I would have said Pilar who? However, that was all about to change.

Chapter 17

PILAR

We're part of the same place.
We're part of the same time.
We both share the same blood.
We both have the same mind.

I was beyond delirious when I received an e-mail from Xavier. He totally and completely made my day and didn't even know it. I was on a natural high, my Xavier high. I did my little happy dance all around my apartment, swaying my hips to the silent music that existed only in my mind.

My immediate thought was to e-mail him back, but then I realized, Xavier was right, life is too short. Sometimes, you had to follow your heart and sometimes that involved drastic measures. I decided I had a plan that would be much better than an e-mail from me. My surprise would be the best ever, and I could hardly wait until it all came together. I couldn't wait to see his expression when it was finally revealed.

Weeks flew by in a blur. I was busy with so little time and so much to do. One thing I didn't do was to e-mail Xavier. My surprise would make up for the lack of communication when it was all completed. I could barely contain myself. I was so excited.

Finally, by the first of October, I was set. My plan was in motion. The weather was crisp and clean. A nice chill permeated the evening air. Football and sweater weather. My favorite time of the year. Packed boxes were all over my apartment, from floor to ceiling. I wasn't aware I had accumulated so much stuff in four short years. When I first moved to Atlanta from Baltimore, I pretty much arrived with the clothes on my back. Atlanta was a fresh start, a new beginning.

The moving truck would be at my apartment in a half hour, and I'd be on a plane just a few short hours later. I had already sold my car and had a new one waiting for me when I touched down at the airport. The salesman was going to meet me with keys in hand. The contracts had already been signed and faxed back and forth.

Yes, it was official; I was moving to Houston! I was so excited about my move I could barely stand still. Atlanta was okay, but I had always wanted to live in Texas after watching the TV show *Dallas* back in the day. Fortunately for me, because I was a freelance writer, I could live anywhere because I could write from anywhere.

I had handled my entire move over the phone and Internet. I was renting an apartment not too far from where Xavier lived. I couldn't be too far from my man. I had seen photos of it over the Internet and fell in love with the apartment community. The apartment itself appeared nice and cozy. There were actually three bedrooms and I could use one as an office.

I was so happy about starting a new life in Houston. A new life with Xavier. It was a new dawn. It was a new day. It was a new life for me. I was feeling good and no one could tell me that Xavier and I wouldn't be together soon. And forever. *Happy, happy, happy dance.*

I had been in Houston for two weeks. I spent most of that time learning the city and getting familiar with my new surroundings. Houston was the fourth largest city in the country, but still had a small, Southern flavor to it. It wasn't that much different from Atlanta. The interstates and streets drove me crazy though. The street signs and markers were definitely for someone who knew where he or she was going in the city. I got lost so many times trying to get around, but eventually driving became easier.

The very first night, I drove by Xavier's home and thought my heart was going to beat out of my chest. Just the thought of being so close to him, breathing the same air, almost gave me heart palpitations. I knew then I couldn't wait much longer before I saw him.

Xavier lived in the sort of house I imagined he would. He owned a two-story, with basement, traditional brick with a perfectly manicured lawn and shrubbery. It was obvious he had someone to care for it. From the outside, everything looked picture perfect. I sat in my car for over two hours, parked down from his house, and just imagined myself inside, as his woman, cuddled up next to him in bed, his arms around my waist. Shortly before dawn, I crept away.

Standing in the checkout line at the Starbucks café located inside Borders, I adjusted the white plastic bag that contained the two books I had purchased, and pulled my wallet out of my purse to pay for the small, steaming French vanilla cappuccino. When I woke up this morning, I decided it was going to be a "me" day, no writing, no cleaning, no unpacking, nada. I sensed a tinge of excitement in the air. Something fabulous was going to happen. I sensed it with every ounce of my being.

I had walked over to one of the mini circular tables in the far corner of the café, over near the huge storefront windows that faced out into the mall. A few girls that looked like college students and other early birds were already situated with their laptops propped open, doing whatever they came there to do. Suddenly, I heard someone quietly call my name.

"Pilar?"

I slowly turned in the direction of the familiar voice, the one that invaded my dreams, and I instantly smiled. A huge Kool-Aid smile.

"Xavier. Hi," I whispered, waving timidly.

He walked over and we were facing each other. Every time I saw him, he took my breath away. Today was no different. There were a few awkward seconds when neither one of us knew what to say because a lot had occurred between us. We had a history now. I was the first to break eye contact by looking down at the floor.

"Wow! We've got to stop meeting like this," Xavier jokingly said and smiled, showing those deep dimples again and perfect white teeth. "What are you doing in my neck of the woods?"

Xavier was as handsome as I remembered. He was wearing blue jeans, a sweatshirt and tennis shoes. I think this was the first time I had ever seen him this dressed down. He'd be fine in anything; even wearing some dirty drawers, scratching his butt. I noticed he had a laptop bag draped on his shoulder.

"I'm temporarily in town, working on a documentary I plan to eventually film."

"Really?" he asked, looking at me like he didn't believe me for one second.

"Yes. I plan to interview Houston residents who moved here after Hurricane Katrina and talk about how their lives were forever changed."

"Sounds interesting. Houston definitely has a large post-Katrina population. "

I nodded my head in agreement. Xavier was still staring at me as if he was unsure if he should be talking with me or running in the opposite direction. I knew he didn't trust me.

I motioned for him to have a seat at my table.

"What are you doing here," I asked.

"Oh, this is one of my writing spots. Sometimes, when I don't want to be cooped up inside, I come here and write through the afternoon. On occasion, they've even had to lock the doors and throw me out when I stayed past closing time. Especially during this time of the year."

"Wow! What a coincidence," I said. "We always seem to run into each other. Our paths were meant to cross."

"Yeah, it is quite a coincidence," Xavier said, giving me a funny look. "I'm not so sure about our paths crossing being divine intervention though."

"Listen, about all that stuff I said in the past . . ."

"No. Pilar, let's not even go there. Don't worry about it," he stated, holding up his hand.

"Please, I'd like to explain and apologize for my comments and actions. It's been bothering me."

Xavier didn't try to stop me this time. He leaned back in his chair and let me purge my feelings. My words tumbled forth.

"I am truly sorry about those horrible things I said to you. Most people would never know I have a horrible temper, but I do. I wasn't myself that day and I understand that's not an excuse. I should have simply respected your wishes and not taken it as a rejection."

"Is that what you thought? I wasn't rejecting you, Pilar."

"I know that now. I've done a lot of thinking about all that went down and now realize I was wrong. Very wrong. You told me up front what was what. I just refused to hear it, I guess."

"Pilar, you are a beautiful, intelligent, articulate woman, but our timing was off from the beginning. I'm engaged to be married. Maybe if I had met you a few years earlier, who knows."

For a flash of a second, my smile completely disappeared. I knew Xavier had a girlfriend; however, I didn't know I was dealing with a fiancée. This was going to be harder to fix than I thought. A girlfriend was one thing, but a soon-to-be wife was on a whole other level. Damn!

"Well, congratulations," I said with the most excitement I could muster and make it sound convincing. "When is the big day?"

"We haven't set a date yet. My fiancée is finishing up law

school, then she has to pass the bar and of course, my new release just dropped. We both have very busy schedules."

"Yeah, I'm sure you have a lot on your plate and there shouldn't be a rush. If the love is there, it will be there six, nine months from now."

"True."

"Anyway, I just wanted the opportunity to explain. Didn't want you to think I was a straight up bitch or, as you said, 'a straight up psycho bitch.'"

He coyly smiled at that. He didn't comment.

"Bottom line, I got caught up and let my emotions get in the way. I'm sorry," I said as sincerely as possible.

"Like I explain in my books, women are emotional creatures and usually they can't separate love from sex. They equate one with the other. Men, on the other hand, have no problem distinguishing between the two," Xavier said like I was his student.

"I guess there is a lot of truth in that. Do you accept my apology?" I asked, not really feeling his college 101 psychoanalysis of my emotions. How did he know what I was feeling?

"I have to ask you one question before I answer," Xavier said, suddenly looking very serious.

"Sure, ask away."

"Did you send my fiancée a text message telling her about us sleeping together in Atlanta?"

"What? No way. No, I didn't," I said, staring him straight in the eyes. "How would I even know her or where to send it? I'd never do any jacked up shit like that."

Xavier didn't respond.

"Maybe someone saw us together at the conference, going into your room, and decided to tell her," I said like I had just solved the mystery.

A few seconds passed. "Okay, I guess I believe you, and I also accept your apology."

"Thank you. That means a lot to me," I said.

"Do you accept mine? I said some crazy shit to you, too."

"Of course I do. That's what friends do, forgive and forget."
I didn't mention that I was willing to forgive, but I wasn't
going to ever forget. Not ever.

"Cool," Xavier said.

"Since we have that out of the way, give me a hug, man," I
said, standing up.

Xavier stood up hesitantly and wrapped his strong arms
around me. I welcomed the closeness and leaned my head
against his chest and breathed him in. Being in his arms felt so
right and so good. The embrace was broken all too soon. I
think I still made him a bit uncomfortable.

"I tell you what. I have some shopping to do, but why don't
I drop back by around lunchtime and take you out to lunch," I
said.

"I don't know," Xavier stated. "I usually write through
lunchtime when I come here."

"Oh, come on. Take a break, Xavier. Quit being so unbend-
ing. You need to eat sometime. Lunch will keep up your
strength and you'll be even more creative."

"I don't know. I probably shouldn't."

"My treat," I said sweetly, looking up at him and thinking,
*This man is so fine. Lord, help me. I can't wait to get some more of
that.*

"No promises, but drop back by when you finish shopping,
I'll see how my writing flow is going and I'll decide then."

"Fair enough. See you in a few," I said, placing a hand gently on his arm.

I left Xavier sitting there, pulling out his laptop as I made
my way into the main section of the three-level mall. I figured
I'd waste a few hours, maybe pick up some sexy lingerie, get a
manicure and pedicure, and then stop back by as he suggested.
I was pretty sure Xavier was going to have lunch with me because he didn't say no when he had the opportunity.

* * *

Three hours later, I arrived back at Starbucks. Xavier was deep in writing mode, the expression on his face was as if he was in another world; he didn't even sense a few women staring and whispering about him. I observed him for a few moments from a distance. He was such a handsome man with rugged features, like a real man was supposed to have. He was not a pretty boy, Shemar Moore type, but a handsome, tall, dark and sexy man. One who amazingly made me wet from a mere hug or touch of his hand. His smile alone took me there.

Xavier was so caught up in his craft, he didn't even see or hear me come up on him. I placed my hand on the small of his neck, let it linger there for a moment. Felt the pulse of his lifeline pump against my fingers.

"Hey, man, you ready?"

He hesitated. Attempted to write that last fleeting sentence.

"Don't give me that bullshit that you work through lunch. Everybody has to eat, including fine men such as yourself."

"I do believe you are flirting with me," he said. I finally had his full attention.

"You think so," I said and winked. "Is there anything wrong with a woman flirting with a handsome man?"

"Absolutely not."

"'Cause if there is, I guess you'll just have to spank me later," I whispered into his ear.

His expression was priceless. I think his dick went instantly hard right then and there, on the spot. He stopped thinking with one head and started thinking with another in that instant.

"We can check out one of my favorite restaurants that I saw driving in, just up the street." I didn't mention that it was conveniently right next door to a hotel.

"You drive a hard bargain, lady."

"Plus, I'd like your opinion on the documentary."

"My opinion? I don't know anything about filming a documentary. I didn't go to film school," he said.

"Neither did I, but I did take a couple of classes years ago. Wanted to do something more serious as opposed to writing fluff pieces for the rest of my life. Anyway, outlining a novel has to be similar."

"Okay, okay. You are relentless. You talked me into it," he stated, holding up his hands in surrender.

Gotcha.

Chapter 18

XAVIER

Damaged goods.

Don't ask me how I went against everything I said I would not do and ended up at a restaurant with Pilar. We were seated at a booth, not an inch of space between us.

She was such a mysterious woman with those big doe-like eyes and wild, crazy hair; I found myself pushing it out of her face several times during our meal. Whatever perfume she was wearing was very sexy; kind of like the outfit she was wearing. Pilar had on a flaming red wraparound dress that hit right above her knees, black tights and boots with two-inch heels. Sexy.

Believe it or not, lunch was fun after I let my guard down. I actually had a decent time. We talked and it wasn't forced, just very natural like we had known each other much longer than we had. Well, let's keep it real. I really didn't know Pilar. The Pilar I knew was the one I fucked. The one whose moans drove me crazy when I was sexing her and hitting the spot.

This Pilar talked about her love of writing from a journalistic perspective. It moved her to show the world the real view of real people living real lives. All that Hollywood glamour shit, that wasn't real life; not even one-quarter of the population lived such a lavish lifestyle. I soon found out Pilar had a passion for showing the world the faces of poverty and suffering and the harsh realities that a percentage of the country suffered each and every day. That was admirable. Somewhere, behind her passionate words, I sensed there was a reason close to home for that drive and passion. Somewhere, deep within the carefully crafted facade she wore, I sensed a damaged woman.

Pilar didn't talk much about her childhood and I didn't pry. She did mention an aunt that appeared to bring a genuine smile to her face. When I tried to ask more about her parents, she changed the subject. I even found myself opening up to her, telling her personal things about myself, like how one of my deepest fears was that I wouldn't be able to provide for myself. So, I pushed, pushed, and pushed myself. I worked hard, played harder, and felt that time was of the essence. I always heard my internal time clock tick, tick, ticking away.

I could understand why she must be an excellent interviewer. Pilar knew how to make people let their guard down, relax and talk about themselves, revealing personal details. I had never really talked to anyone about my fears. Everyone in my life leaned on me for guidance; I was the strong pillar of support. I wasn't supposed to have any fears.

When Pilar talked briefly about her past, however, it was always with a sense of detachment. It was as if she were describing events and happenings that happened to someone else. There was always an air of sadness in her eyes that never quite reached the fake smile on her lips.

Before I knew it, over two hours had passed. Our waitress stopped by our table and asked if we wanted dessert.

"Well, Miss Pilar, are we eating dessert?" I asked, looking from our waitress back to Pilar.

She laughed, drew back her head. "Yes. I declared today as

all about me day. So yes, I am spoiling myself. Strawberry cheesecake for me, please," she said like she was making a major announcement. "What's your pleasure, babe?" she asked with hidden meaning.

"Make that two," I said to the blonde-haired waitress, who wrote our choices down on her pad and walked off to attend to her other tables.

"I'll be right back. I have to go to the restroom," Pilar stated, standing up.

The entire time Pilar was gone, not more than ten minutes, I kept telling myself over and over again that I was going to finish up dessert, have her take me back to my car, and leave it at that. I was not going to take her back to a hotel and fuck her silly like I wanted to do right about now. I even thought about quickly calling up Dré. I knew he would talk me out of doing what I was seriously thinking about. He'd have my back and bring me back to my senses, which had obviously fled.

"Hey, I'm back. You miss me?" she asked, sitting down.

"I kept your spot warm."

"Warm? Don't you know by now, I like it hot?" she teased, licking her lips suggestively.

The waitress brought our cheesecake out with two forks, and Pilar was back under me, with no space separating us, not an inch.

"This has been so much fun today that for the life of me, I can't understand why we fought." As she said this, she reached for my hand and placed it in her lap.

She leaned over and whispered in my ear, "I'm not wearing any panties. When I went into the restroom, I pulled them off and my tights, put them in my purse."

Pilar pulled up her dress a bit to prove her point; no one but myself could see what was going on because of the way the table was situated. She was completely hidden except for my eyes only.

I coughed loudly as I took in the sight of her naked, bikini-waxed pussy. I looked at Pilar's face, and she looked totally amused at my discomfort. I attempted to move my hand, but she reached for it again and placed it back in her lap.

She leaned over close to my ear. "Play with my pussy, babe. It still belongs to you."

If my dick was hard earlier, now it was like a brick.

"She has missed your touch. Been having withdrawal symptoms."

As I stuck a finger inside her, Pilar took a bite of her dessert. "Hmmm, this is so good. Isn't it, babe? All moist and sweet. Melts in your mouth. Want a taste?"

She leaned over and gently nibbled on my earlobe. "I'm all wet for you."

"You are too much." I laughed.

"I want more. Give me more, babe."

I obliged by sticking another digit deep inside her and swirled it around. She opened her legs farther apart so that I had easier access.

"You are making me crazy," she said, taking another bite of cake. I started moving my fingers around, in and out of her womanhood, and Pilar started making these moaning sounds, barely audible, real light. "I'm so wet. Only you can get me like this, babe. All riled up."

About that time, out of the corner of my eye, I saw our waitress headed back over to our table. Oh shit! I tried to quickly remove my hand, but Pilar crossed her legs and trapped my fingers inside her.

"Is everything okay over here?" the waitress asked, smiling sweetly, working for her tip now.

"Wonderful," Pilar answered for the both of us. "We just need the check, please."

"Okay, give me five minutes and I'll bring it right back."

After the waitress left, we looked at each other and burst out laughing hysterically.

"You are a bad girl, you know that?" I said, moving her hair out of her face.

"I am. You are going to have to give me a good spanking. I've been very bad today."

I nodded my head and smiled.

Taking her hand and placing it on my dick, I said, "See what you made me do? Got my shit all hard."

"I'm sorry. I'll have to come up with some way to make it go back down," she said naughtily.

"I'll think of something."

"I bet you will," she said.

She leaned over to kiss me lightly on the lips and I didn't resist. I kissed her back, inserting my tongue in her mouth.

"Babe, we have a few minutes before the waitress comes back. Think you can make me come?"

"Is that a challenge?" I asked.

"Call it what you want. I just want to come all over your fingers."

"You're a nasty girl."

"You are wasting time," she whispered.

That was my signal to get to work. I had always been like that. I had no problem with putting in work to get my woman off, any woman off. That's just the way I was taught: always satisfy the woman first, before you got yours. My fingers were all up in her, stroking her clit, going in and out, deeper and deeper. Whispering nasty shit in her ear:

"How does that feel?" I asked.

"If you think that feels good, can you imagine how my dick will feel going up inside you?"

I said, "When I get you alone, I'm going to tear that ass up."

"Damn, you got some good pussy, baby."

"You ready to come? Come for daddy. Give it up."

Just as the waitress was walking toward our table, I felt Pilar start to tremble and shake.

"That's right. Let it go. That's my girl," I whispered in her ear. "Let it go for daddy. Umm-huh, that's it."

She started breathing rapidly and leaned into my arm. She

let out one big moan, which made the brother sitting directly parallel to us look in my direction and give me a nod, like oh yeah, get her off. He knew the real deal.

Just as the waitress made it back to the table, Pilar came all over my fingers and I felt her warm liquid dripping down my index finger as I pulled out.

"Here you go. Come back and see us now," the waitress said, none the wiser as she laid the check on the table in front of me.

"We will."

"Is she okay?" she asked, looking at Pilar, who was resting against me like she couldn't move, with her eyes halfway closed.

"Yeah, she's just tired."

"Oh, well, get her home and into bed," the waitress stated.

"I will."

After Pilar and I cleaned ourselves up in the restrooms, left a huge tip, we couldn't wait to get up out of there. We didn't even have to ask one another. We went straight to the hotel next door and registered.

On the elevator ride up to the tenth floor, we almost tore each other's clothes off. Lucky for us, no one else got on the elevator. I had my finger inside her again, her leg propped up on my arm, while I freed her breast from her dress and sucked her nipple. It was the longest walk to the room in the back corner.

As soon as I managed to open the door and step inside the room, we were stripping off clothes, kissing, and all over one another like animals in heat. Hungry for each other's touch. Her hands were like fire as they touched my bare skin. The sex turned out to be some of the most exciting I have ever had, and I've had a lot of sexual encounters, so that's saying a lot. There was just something about Pilar. She did it for me. Sexually. On an emotional level she was too needy and clingy. That was the problem. She wanted to own me, and I wasn't having that.

"Get over here and take care of this hard on I've had since I walked through Starbucks and saw you," I commanded.

She attempted to get on the bed.

"No, not on the bed. I want you on your knees," I said, now standing in the middle of the floor.

By now, we were both buck naked, and Pilar got on her knees and started giving me a blowjob. I held the back of her head to make sure she took all of me. She only gagged a few times as she smoothly slid my tool in and out of her mouth.

"Oh yeah. Damn! Oh yeah, baby," I said. "That's right."

This went on for a while before I yanked her away and sort of tossed her on the bed.

"Spread your legs."

She obliged.

"Wider."

I climbed to the side of her on the bed, stroked her clit with my finger for a few minutes and reached up and tweaked her nipples really hard, both at the same time. They were rock hard and erect.

"Oh, don't!" she screamed.

I licked my tongue across both nipples, got them slippery wet, glistening with my saliva and I tweaked them again.

"No, stop! That hurts," she screamed, trying to cover up her breasts. I hit her hands away.

I really don't know what got into me. I enjoyed sex and had probably tried every sexual position known and even made up a few of my own. I was never into S&M or role-playing, but for some reason, I felt the urge to punish Pilar.

I don't know if I wanted to punish her because I couldn't get enough of her. Punish her for making me weak for her. Punish her for making me betray Kendall. Punish her for making me do things that were out of my nature. I don't know. I just knew I wanted to hurt her and that scared me. I wanted to bring her pain. Pain that turned into pleasure.

I put my fingers back inside her and bit down on her right nipple.

"Oh, please stop! No! No! No!" she screamed.

"You know you like it."

I flipped her over onto her stomach.

Slapping her ass, I said, "Say you like it."

She didn't say anything. Looked back at me with a bit of confusion.

I slapped that ass two more times, harder this time. I know it hurt her because I saw the red mark that instantly appeared.

"Say it!" I demanded, pulling her by the hair to face me. I stuck my tongue almost down her throat. Made her kiss me.

She opened her mouth to say something.

"I can't hear you." I smacked that ass again.

"Yes! Yes, I like it!"

"Say you love it."

"I love it."

"That's better. Now get on your knees."

She slowly rose to her knees.

I palmed her cheeks, rubbing and stroking my hands across her ass. Then, out of the blue, without warning, I slapped her cheeks again. My hand hitting flesh broke the silence in the room.

As she tried to pull away from me, Pilar almost cried out for me to stop, then she caught herself.

"Do you want me to fuck you?"

"Yes."

"Yes, what?"

"Yes, I want you to fuck me."

"Say, please."

"Please fuck me, babe."

For the next hour, we did exactly that. She tried pulling away several times, but I'd pull her right back. Into the pain that turned to pleasure. Much like our relationship.

Around midnight, I was almost out for the count; sleep seductively calling my name. Pilar, with her head on my shoulder, slightly snoring, was already sound asleep. Dead tired. I had literally worn her out. Earlier, I had ordered room service. We had eaten pizza and drank a bottle of wine before another round of sex. Then, we watched a movie on HBO like a normal couple would do. Normal was not even close to describing us.

I lay there for a while, with this woman I really didn't know, wrapped up in my arms. What the hell was I doing? Why was I drawn to her? Better yet, why was she drawn to me? What was the fatal attraction?

In the wee hours, somewhere between darkness and dawn, I was awakened from a deep slumber. At first, I thought I was dreaming; I heard crying, coming from what appeared to be far, far away. Then, I thought maybe it was a toddler in another room on the floor. When I finally woke up completely and looked around at my surroundings, I realized it was coming from inside my own room.

I sat up abruptly when I realized Pilar wasn't in bed with me. I turned on the lamp on the nightstand, trying to adjust my eyes to the light that pierced through the darkness. When I looked to my left, I saw her curled up on the floor, with her hands wrapped around her knees, rocking slowly back and forth. Back and forth. Trancelike. Still had on my shirt, which completely swallowed her. She looked like a helpless, frightened little girl.

"Pilar?" I called out, getting up to walk over to her. Oblivious to my nakedness.

She didn't answer. Continued to rock back and forth and cry big, heart-wrenching tears that fell to the carpeted floor.

I thought maybe I had hurt her earlier. Confusion flooded me.

"I won't do it again. I'm sorry," she sobbed in a babylike voice that sounded nothing like her own.

The sound stopped me in my tracks.

"I promise. I'll be a good girl. I won't be bad. I won't be bad. I promise. I'll be your good, sweet girl."

"Pilar?"

I walked up and gently placed my hand on her shoulder and she started screaming, "I'll be good. I don't want to be punished. No!" she screamed again, attempting to scoot away. "I don't want to go in the room. Not there. I won't tell. I promise."

"Pilar, it's okay. It's me, Xavier. You are having a nightmare," I gently stated, bending down to look at her, into her eyes. "You are just having a nightmare."

She was in another world. Had no idea she was in a hotel room in Houston. Had no idea she was revealing dark secrets to a stranger. She was in another place and time.

"Pilar, it's going to be all right."

Her blank, crazed stare scared the hell out of me. Chilled me to the bone.

"Pilar, come back to bed," I said gently. "No one is going to hurt you."

She started to rock even more, sobbing, with her thumb in her mouth. The sound was something I will never forget. So much pain. So much despair. Pure helplessness. Sorrow cloaked her like a wrap.

When my shirt fell down off her shoulders, I saw all the bruises I had placed on her during our rough sex play. There were even bruises on her thighs. Suddenly, I felt ashamed that I had hurt this woman/child. I got down on the floor, held her, and rocked her in my arms until she calmed down. Twenty minutes later, the sobbing ceased and I literally carried her back to bed. She instantly drifted back into a hard, fretful sleep. She tossed and turned most of the night.

In no time at all, she reached for me and found her way back into my arms, even in sleep. I held her protectively through most of the early morning. My mind was reeling. I finally drifted off with the knowledge that somebody had seriously hurt Pilar in the past.

Chapter 19

PILAR

Let the games begin.

I arose the next morning to find Xavier sitting up in bed, at my side, caressing my cheek and pushing my hair out of my face. He was touching me like he cared. For the first time, I saw a softer side to him.

"Hi," I said with a dry, parched throat.

"Hi, yourself," he said. "How are you feeling this morning?"

I attempted to sit up and an ache shot through my body.

"I think we overdid it with the rough sex last night, huh?" he said, seeing my physical discomfort.

"I think so. I'm definitely sore."

"I didn't realize I was being so rough. Here, take this," he stated as he handed me two Tylenol and a glass of water from the nightstand.

"Thanks. You really can be sweet when you want to," I kidded as I threw my head back to swallow the tablets and take a gulp of water.

"Do you remember anything from last night?" Xavier asked.

"Yeah, I remember the incredible sex."

"No, I don't mean . . ."

"What?" I asked curiously.

He hesitated. "Nothing. Never mind."

"No. What?" I asked again.

"Nothing. Do you know you snore in your sleep?"

"I do not."

"Yes, you do. I thought a big ole grizzly bear was sleeping next to me. It's not exactly sexy."

I laughed and looked at him, reached for his hand and kissed the inside of his palm. "What are we going to do today?"

"I don't know about you, but I'm going to go home and write. Make up for the time I lost yesterday."

"Oh, I just thought . . ."

"Thought what?" he asked, standing up to pull on his pants that had been lying on the back of a chair, neatly folded.

"Forget it. Just wishful thinking."

At that moment, his cell phone vibrated. He checked the caller ID.

"Damn!"

"What? What's wrong?"

"That was Kendall."

"Who's Kendall, babe?"

"My fiancée."

"Oh." That was all I could muster at that moment.

"She has blown my phone up since last night," he said, checking his missed messages. "Listen, I got to get out of here. Damn!"

I was secretly smiling, hoping he would get busted.

"Get dressed so we can get out of here. I need my shirt back and for you to drive me back to my car."

"Oh, sure," I said, rising to walk into the bathroom for a shower.

"Make it quick."

"Okay."

"Pilar?"

"Yes?" I asked, stopping and turning to face him.

"I'm happy we came to an understanding regarding our arrangement."

"Yeah, me too," I said matter-of-factly.

"It makes this easier."

I nodded.

"Are you all right?" he asked, looking at me curiously.

"Just fine. Couldn't be better." Those words couldn't be further from the truth. Inside, I was simmering, slowly coming to an angry boil.

I took a quick shower and put on my clothes from the day before. Nothing had changed. Going back down in the elevator was definitely different than it had been coming up the day before. Driving back to Xavier's car, we were both quiet, lost in thought. Nothing had changed; Xavier still didn't love me. Couldn't see past the sex. To him, I was a booty call, plain and simple. Nothing more. He didn't care about me.

I pulled up next to Xavier's car. He leaned over and kissed me full on the lips.

I simply looked at him. I couldn't believe that once again he was running back to her.

"Pilar, take care of yourself and thanks for last night," he said, turning toward me.

There was that shit again. *"Thank you?" Don't thank me. Tell me you enjoyed my company and you'd like to see me again. Tell me that, not some thank you shit.* Did he tell his woman thank you every time they were intimate? Hell, no!

"You're welcome," I replied dryly.

Xavier reached for the doorknob to open his door, then hesitated. I held my breath.

"Listen, give me your cell number. I'll call you if I have a free moment to discuss the documentary. I'm not making any promises though."

Of course not, I thought. Xavier could never make me a promise. That would be asking too much on his end. Giving too much of himself.

I gave him my number, watched him get into his car and drive away without looking back once. Not once. Just that quickly I was out of his mind. Out of sight, out of mind.

I now knew as clearly as day what I needed to do. I definitely needed to check out my competition. If I was going to come out the ultimate winner in this game, I had to know who and what I was up against. I couldn't wait to meet Miss Kendall. Let the games begin.

Chapter 20

XAVIER

Too close for comfort.

Ten o'clock. Good. Dré would be in the office by now. I quickly dialed his work number as I merged onto the interstate. Luckily for me, rush hour traffic was over, which meant one less thing for me to deal with.

Dré picked up, speaking in his professional banker's tone.

"Dré, I need you to cover for me, man."

"Hold up. Slow down for a minute."

"Sorry, man. My head is not on straight right now."

"What's up?"

"I hooked up with her again."

"Hooked up with who?"

"The Pilar chick I told you about."

"Oh, man, no you didn't."

"I'm afraid I did."

"You are one hard-headed mofo. The last time we talked I warned you about this chick. I have a bad feeling about her."

"Save your 'I told you so' for a minute. I need you to cover for me, all right?"

"You know I got your back. What's up?" he said.

"Kendall has been blowing up my cell since last night. She even called a few minutes ago."

"Man, what were you thinking? You know the rules. You can't change your routine in mid-stream. If you speak with your woman every day, you can't suddenly not call her or be unavailable. That's a dead giveaway."

"I know. I know. I just got so caught up with this chick."

"Yeah, sounds like you were thinking with the other head and not the one that sits on your neck. This chick must have gold between her legs. Platinum pussy."

"Listen, if Kendall asks when you see her again, I need you to tell her I was with you last night. That I crashed at your pad after we went out drinking."

"Okay, cool. Like I said, I got your back. No worries."

"You got it? The story?"

"Yeah. I'm cool."

"I'll talk to you later and give you the details about what went down, but now, I have to make a phone call."

"Go handle your business, playa. Handle your business."

A few minutes later, I pulled into my driveway and rolled up into my garage. I dialed Kendall's cell as I walked through the garage door into my kitchen.

"Hello?"

"Hey, baby."

"Don't hey, baby me," she said, sounding totally pissed as I had expected.

"Where have you been? I've been trying to reach you since last night, Xavier. I was so worried. Didn't know what happened."

"Calm down, baby. Relax. I'm fine."

"Don't tell me to calm down. Where have you been, Xavier?"

"I just walked in the house."

"From where? Where have you been all night?"

"I crashed at Dré's last night."

"Why? You never stay over there."

"Usually I don't, but last night was like old times. Dré closed a huge deal at work, so we went out to celebrate. One drink led to another, then another, and before we knew it we were both a little drunk."

"Uh-huh."

"Dré lived the closest to the bar so we drove back there. Once I managed to stumble into his house, I crashed on his sofa until this morning. I didn't trust trying to drive myself home."

"I tried calling all night. Why didn't you pick up your cell phone?"

"Baby, I just saw your messages. Earlier, when I went over to Dré's house, I must have laid my phone down and forgot it when we left because I didn't find it until this morning, stuffed between the cushions of his sofa."

"You're just getting home?"

"Yes. I drank entirely too much. Have a killer headache now. I'm going to take some Tylenol and lay back down."

"Poor baby," she purred. "That's what you get for acting like some out of control college student."

"Those days are long gone for me. I'll leave the college student stuff to you."

"Whatever. Well, get some rest."

"I will, but I'd be happier if you were laying down beside me, with your head on my chest."

"Me too. But you know I have class."

"I know, but I'll dream of you."

"You'd better, and don't you ever scare me like that again. Do you hear me?"

"I won't. I promise. Were you really scared?"

"I didn't know what had happened. All kinds of crazy thoughts went through my mind."

"I bet they did." I laughed.

"Seriously, sweetie."

"What? You thought I was laid up somewhere, screwing some woman?" I asked jokingly.

"You laugh. It did cross my mind."

"How many times have I told you how much I love you?"

"Too many to count."

"Do you believe me?" I asked. "Don't you trust me?"

"Of course, sweetie. You know I do."

"Good. Because you know I'd never do anything to intentionally hurt you."

"I know, man. It doesn't hurt to hear you say it though."

"Okay, I'm going to take this Tylenol and hit the sack."

"Okay, sweetie. Call me later."

"I will," I said.

"Talk to you later then."

"Kendall?"

"Yes?"

"I love you, baby."

"Love you more."

Right before I drifted off to sleep, I said a silent prayer that Kendall believed me because I didn't want to lose the best thing that had ever happened to me simply because I couldn't keep my dick in my pants.

Three hours later, I bolted upright from a deep slumber in which I dreamed Pilar and I were laying in bed. She leaned over and whispered seductively in my ear, "Xavier, let me taste you." Just as she was about to open her mouth, she pulled out a huge butcher knife and chopped off my dick. I woke up drenched in a cold sweat.

Chapter 21

PILAR

*W*ho's *playing tricks?*

After my last rendezvous with Xavier, I spent the next couple of weeks getting to know Kendall. From a distance, of course. I didn't want to play my hand, not yet anyway. *Rule of Engagement #1: Know your enemy's strengths and weaknesses before you launch an attack.* And right now, Kendall was my number one enemy. I had all the time in the world to watch and learn. Patience was one of my best virtues.

It was really quite easy. Almost too simple. It didn't take much effort on my part to obtain Kendall's home address, landline, and of course, I already had her cell phone number. I was going to have fun with that, too.

Speaking of Xavier, he didn't attempt to call me. I figured he wouldn't. No surprise there. I sent him an e-mail maybe twice a week, one on Monday and one on Friday, to keep our connection intact and insure he kept me in his thoughts. He'd respond in his typical one-word or two-word answer and act as if I was seriously intruding on his space and precious time. Sometimes, he simply wouldn't respond at all. That pissed me off so much. It showed a total lack of respect for me, yet I kept

coming back based on the times when he did show me his undivided attention. I was never intruding when I was on my
knees for him. He didn't totally realize what his lack of interest
did to me. I don't think he cared.

Getting back to Kendall, the silly bitch never even knew
she was being followed. One time, I was only two customers
behind her in line at a fast food restaurant. I had the opportunity to check her out, and I'll be the first to admit that she was
a lovely woman. I wouldn't expect less of Xavier. He had an
eye for stunning women and wouldn't have anything else on
his arm.

Kendall had a natural beauty about herself. She mostly kept
her long black hair pulled back in a neat ponytail and wore
very little makeup, yet was very beautiful with her long legs
and dancer-like frame.

It's funny how people aren't very observant of their surroundings or the people in their space, and I've found that
most people are creatures of habit. We drive the same route to
work, around the same time, every day. We eat at the same
restaurants, order the same food items, work out at the same
gym, go to the same grocery store, dry cleaners, drug store, day
in and day out. Creatures of habit. Big mistake.

Being a college student in law school, Kendall's schedule
was even easier to follow. So, Xavier liked them young? For the
life of me, I couldn't figure out why he'd want a young woman
still in her late twenties, as opposed to a thirty-something
woman like myself, who had seen and done a few things in life.
Sure, Kendall was smart, she was forever studying at that damn
library, but that didn't mean she was rich in life experience.
That came only with age. There's something to be said for
shared highs and lows in life. Being part of the same genera-
tion. Sharing relatable events.

Into my third week of following her, on Wednesday, I noticed Kendall left campus a little earlier than usual and drove
to a very familiar location. I silently fumed inside as I passed

his house and circled around the block, twice. By the time I made my way back and parked a couple of cars down the street, I witnessed Xavier opening the door for Kendall. They kissed passionately and he led her inside with his arms around her waist, nuzzling her neck.

I sat in my car for over two hours and literally saw red. Fuming, I pummeled my fist on the steering wheel again and again until they were bloody and raw. I didn't feel any pain. My world consisted of a thick cloud of red that expressed my jealousy and rage. I knew what was going on inside that house. I thought about creeping around back to peek in a window, but realized that would be too careless in broad daylight. A nosy neighbor might be looking out, watching me. So I waited and waited and waited.

I pulled out my *other* BlackBerry from the dashboard and dialed Kendall's cell. It rang and rang and rang, eventually going into voice mail. I hated that crisp, clipped, cheerful pitch of her voice. I could tell that she had never suffered, had never felt any pain or been made to feel invisible. I bet she always received whatever she wanted, got exactly what she needed. She was privileged and I resented that. Resented that with a passion.

Kendall was not going to have Xavier. He was mine. I don't care if she saw him first. Xavier belonged to me. If he had met me first, he never would have looked twice at her. Kendall was so pathetic to me. She didn't even know how to please him or he wouldn't come running to me every time he needed a fix.

If Xavier had met me first, he would have realized he and I were connected and meant for one another. The chemistry and bond was there. Xavier had to be still and just listen. He couldn't listen with Kendall in his ear. She distracted him. Confused him with her clipped, crisp, chipped chatter.

I dialed her cell phone again. It rang two, three times.

"Pick up, you pathetic bitch," I screamed in fury. "Pick up your damn phone!"

"Hello?" her now familiar voice said. She sounded happy and fulfilled. That's what good loving will do for you.

I wasn't prepared for her to answer, so I was taken aback for a second.

"Hello?"

Complete silence.

"Is anyone there?"

I heard Xavier's deep voice asking her something in the background that I couldn't quite make out.

"I guess it's a wrong number. No one is saying anything and I only hear raspy breathing." I heard her tell Xavier right before she hung up.

I called back again. How dare she hang up on me? Who did she think she was? It rang again and then again.

"Hello?" she asked with annoyance clearly etched in her tone.

"Hello?"

I froze. The masculine voice on the other end threw me for a loop.

"Who is this?" I heard Xavier ask. "Don't call this fucking number again. Quit playing on my fucking phone."

I hung up, trembling.

Thirty minutes later, the front door opened. Kendall had a huge smile on her face. *I bet she did.* Her hair was no longer pulled back in a neat ponytail and she looked disheveled. My blood pressure nearly flew through the roof when Xavier bent down to kiss her and caressed her butt through her skinny jeans.

The bitch almost skipped back to her car. That girl didn't know how to handle a man like Xavier. Didn't even know where to begin. He'd marry her, and after a couple of years, they'd be like strangers living under the same roof, especially after he impregnated her.

Kendall didn't have what it took sexually to keep his interest sated. He'd be back to hitting it in every major market he toured. A different woman in every city. I, on the other hand, knew exactly what it took to please Xavier, and he understood that all too well. Now, I needed to come up with a plan for him to realize he needed me in his life forever. Not just overnight.

"Hi, Leeda?"

"Hi, Pilar. How are you?" she asked.

"I'm fine. I live in Houston now," I said without any preamble.

"Well, I'm glad you are finally telling me. I thought we had a relationship, but you just up and moved to Houston without warning. Didn't think to let me know."

"I'm sorry. It was a move that was done on a whim. I didn't put much thought into it. I made up my mind and did it. You know I can be impulsive at times."

"I see."

"I'm telling you now though," I volunteered. "Don't be upset."

"I'm not," Leeda said.

"Good, because you are the only friend I have."

"Have you seen him yet?"

"Who?" I asked.

"Pilar, don't play coy."

"Xavier?"

"Yes," Leeda said.

"I have."

"And?" Leeda asked.

"And what?"

"Has anything changed since you moved to Houston? Have all your dreams come true?"

"Not really."

"Well, what did you think your move would accomplish, Pilar?"

"I'd be able to spend more time with Xavier and he'd get to know me and eventually love me, want me and need me."

"Has he?"

"No," I said. "I mean nothing to him. Absolutely nothing."

I don't know what overcame me. I burst into tears. I always felt comfortable revealing my feelings to Leeda. She always put me at ease and never judged me because she had definitely seen the worst side of me; the side most people wouldn't want to witness. Most people wouldn't want to be my friend if they knew the real me and what I was capable of. Sometimes it scared me realizing what I was capable of.

For minutes, the phone line was filled with my frustration, angst and tears. And I rarely cried. I had learned years ago that tears brought more pain. It was best to keep emotions balled up inside, away from prying eyes.

"What's wrong with me, Leeda? I give and give and give of myself, but no one ever loves me. I try my hardest to do and say the right things, yet I always wind up hurt. Why can't I find love? Am I that damaged? Fix me."

"What's happened? Why are you crying, Pilar? Calm down, take a deep breath and slowly count to ten."

"Xavier has a fiancée," I revealed in between fresh sobs.

"He told you?"

"Yes. He told me all about her."

"I'm surprised."

"Plus, I've seen them together. She's very pretty, and smart and classy and nothing at all like me."

"Pilar, you have all those qualities and more. I'm so sorry, but I did warn you about Xavier and trying to establish a relationship with him. If a man is interested, he'll let you know. You can't force a relationship."

"Just tell me why I can't find love. Why can't anyone love me?"

"You have to love yourself first. It's that simple. Love yourself first."

"I do."

"Do you really? Think about it. You allow this man to sleep

with you and then go home to his fiancée. Is that loving your-self?"

I didn't answer.

"I have to go. I'll talk to you soon," I said.

With that, I hung up. Didn't even wait for her to say good-bye. She always thought she had the answers. I'd show her. I'd show them all.

Chapter 22

XAVIER

When the cat's away, the mouse will play.

"Drive carefully and call me when you get there, no matter how late it is."

"I will, sweetie. Tell Dré hello for me, and the two of you stay out of trouble. I don't want any repeats of the last time you guys went out drinking."

I turned to Dré. "Kendall said hello."

"Hey, baby girl," he shouted back.

"Did you get those tires rotated like I told you?"

"Yes. Earlier this morning. I went to the mechanic you referred me to."

"Good." Kendall had come outside one morning to find two of her car tires completely flat, for no apparent reason.

"Anything else, Daddy?" she kidded.

"No, I guess that is about it. Let me let you go. Take your time and stop if you get tired or sleepy."

"I will."

"Promise me."

"I promise, sweetie. You are too good to me."

"I love you."

"Love you back," she stated.

With that, Kendall and I hung up. I couldn't contain the goofy smile on my face.

I looked over at Dré, who was staring at me with amusement written clearly across his face. "What?" I asked.

"That girl has your nose wide open."

"Maybe she does. And it feels great."

"Where did you say Kendall's parents live?" Dré asked, distracted by a group of attractive women who had just entered the bar and were now sitting not too far from us.

"They live right outside of Dallas, in a very exclusive neighborhood; she's only going home for the weekend. First time in months."

"I've got to give it to her; that is one focused woman," Dré said. "Very goal-oriented and driven."

"That she is, but this weekend she needed to get away and get the kind of pampering only your mom can give you."

"Why? Is she studying too much and needed a break?"

"Yeah, that too, but mostly because she has been getting these hang-up phone calls on her cell and home number lately that have her stressed out."

"Strange."

"It is strange. The person never says anything, just holds the line and breathes into the phone. Sometimes, as soon as she picks up, the person hangs up," I said.

"You don't think that crazy chick has anything to do with this, do you?" he asked.

"That's what I thought at first, but Pilar and I are finally on the same page. We have an understanding. She knows the deal."

"If you say so. I wouldn't trust her as far as I could throw her. Tell Kendall to change her numbers."

"That's what I told her, and if it doesn't stop, she will change them, but you know what an inconvenience that is. You have to give your new numbers to everybody, and it's just a real hassle. She's hoping that whoever it is, probably some kids, will get tired and stop calling."

"Man, you know you have seven lives," Dré said, taking another swallow of his beer.

"What do you mean?" I asked, taking a gulp of my beer as well and laying my cell phone back on the wooden bar.

"I just knew that shit from a few weeks ago was going to catch up with you. In a major way."

"Well, hang with me, partner, and maybe you'll learn some tricks of the trade."

Dré laughed. "Yeah, whatever. Your ass just got lucky."

"Don't hate. Call it what you want, but all is well in my humble abode."

"It does sound like things are going well," Dré said, looking around, checking out the women across from us again.

"I can't complain. I'm happy, actually happier than I've been in a while, but all relationships have highs and lows. Nothing is ever perfect."

"Who you telling? You are preaching to the choir, man. After two marriages and two divorces, I'm happy with the single life. These women will drive you crazy if you let them. Can't live with them, can't live without them."

"You simply never learned the art of keeping them in check."

"And you have?" he asked.

"Don't play with me, Dré. You know I have never taken shit from any woman I've ever been with. I don't have time for all that drama and chaos in my life. If a chick intends to bring that my way, she'd better get to steppin'."

"What about Miss New Orleans?" Dré started laughing.

"Give me a break. You are never going to let me live that down."

"You're right, I'm not. That was some funny shit. You running around thinking you had some roots on you. Thinking your dick was going to fall off."

"Anyway, as I was saying . . . Kendall and I, we aren't perfect and we each have our imperfections and recognize that."

"I keep waiting for you to get to the punch line."

"No punch line. I'm just saying that Kendall isn't perfect."

"And neither are you," Dré interjected.

I signaled the bartender for another round. Dré and I had been sitting at our favorite sports bar for more than an hour now, mostly drinking, talking shit, sports and women.

"As much as I love her, she isn't aggressive enough for me in the bedroom."

"You'll teach her," Dré said.

"That's what I thought at first too, but I'm not so sure now. She is simply not the freaky type. She mostly lies there and lets me do all the work. I adore classy, intelligent women, but they have to be freaks in the sheets."

"Man, get over it. You've found a beautiful, intelligent woman who loves you and you love her . . . that's all you need. A lot of men would gladly trade places with you. The rest will work its way out."

"I hope so," I stated. "I surely hope so," I said, staring off into space.

Dré pulled me out of my reverie. "Man, check out the chick over to your right. The one in black, with the sexy legs. She's been giving me the eye for the last fifteen minutes."

I discreetly glanced over at who he was talking about.

"I think she wants me, man," he said, laughing. "Been flirting with her eyes."

"Oh, I noticed her earlier when she walked by. She doesn't have enough ass for me."

"My brother, we aren't all ass men. Some of us like big breasts and thighs, sexy legs. My woman doesn't have to have ass for days."

We laughed as brothers do.

"To each his own. Don't let me hold you back. Go get the

digits; I'll be here when you get back. Handle your business, partner."

"I think I will," he said, rising from the barstool.

I sat back and enjoyed the atmosphere. I was a serious sport fanatic and enjoyed all sports, so I was pretty much watching some game throughout the entire year. My eyes focused on the huge TV monitor in front of me, checked out the score, but my mind was elsewhere.

Lately, I couldn't seem to get Pilar off my mind. Throughout my day, without warning, she'd pop into my mind. Mostly flashbacks of us in the throes of passion. There was just something about her that turned me on and made me lose rational reasoning. I don't even think Pilar fully realized just how sexy she was.

I still had the phone number she'd given me our last time together, and was almost tempted to call her the other day. I had dialed the number, and at the very last minute, I hung up. Pilar was too emotionally needy for me. Even though she claimed she would work on separating emotion from our sexapades, I wasn't entirely convinced. If I could just bang her whenever I wanted and walk away, I'd have no qualms, but lately it was getting harder and harder to do that. Pilar was quite the mystery. She confused me, excited me, and made me want to distance myself all at the same time. Later, I'd learn that I should have taken the third option.

Chapter 23

PILAR

Never make someone your priority while allowing yourself to be an option!

I received the shock of my life late Friday night. I was lounging around in an old, dingy T-shirt and underwear, half-watching a reality show on TV. My weekends were dull. Welcome to my world. I didn't have any friends other than Leeda, who was all the way in Georgia, and because I worked from home, I rarely had daily interaction with other adults. Writing is such a solitary occupation. My e-mails to Xavier were the extent of my contact with another adult I knew in the area.

My phone rang and I picked it up without really paying attention to the caller ID, thinking it was a telemarketer. I was so bored I was willing to listen to their sales pitch regarding whatever product or service they were selling. At least it was human contact.

"Hello?"

"Hi, Pilar, this is Xavier."

"I know who you are. I recognize your voice," I said, trying to contain my excitement. This was the first time Xavier had ever made the first contact. My night was looking up.

"How are you?" Xavier said like we had talked just yesterday.

"Bored."

"Well, that's not good on a Friday night. I just returned from the sports bar; met a friend there. How's the documentary coming along?" I could sense he wasn't truly interested; he asked just to keep the conversation flowing.

"Slow, but steady. I can't complain. I'm doing the background work now, and it takes up a lot of my time."

"That's great. Glad to hear. I know you are passionate about doing some serious pieces. I think all writers should leave at least one notable work behind as a legacy."

"How's your manuscript coming along?"

"Actually, great. It's the sequel to *Secret Desires,* and I had always said I'd never write a sequel to any of my novels. Never say never, I guess."

"You know I will be one of the first in line to purchase it when it's released, since I'm your number one fan."

We laughed at that. I sensed Xavier was more comfortable with me now.

"I can't believe I caught you at home on a Friday night. Thought you'd have a hot date or something."

"I told you I don't really date. I'm particular about who I give myself to," I said.

"Yeah, you did share that with me when we first met. What's special about me? Why do you give yourself so freely to me? I'm curious."

"I can't believe you are asking me that," I said, making myself comfortable on the sofa.

"I want to know. I've never met a woman quite like you before. You are an original, a bit mysterious." I could tell that he was serious with his questions.

I laughed again.

"Ditto. I've never met a man like you before," I said in return.

"Seriously, tell me. Why me?"

"It's simple. I like you, I truly like you, and I feel such a strong connection to you, like I've never felt with another man before. I realize it sounds totally off the wall, pretty corny. It's like I've been waiting for you my entire life and I didn't even know it until I found you. I want to be with you, spend time with you, get to know you, never let go. That makes me happy. You make me happy. Now that you're here, now that I've found you, you don't even want me, and that makes me sad."

"Wow. That's deep," he said, sounding like what I said was unbelievable.

"That's all you can say?" I asked, turning over on my back, staring up at the off-white ceiling.

"I like you. Why can't that be enough? I mean, what can I say after that declaration? I mean, I'm definitely flattered, very, but you know my situation."

"I sure do. You remind me every chance you get," I said with a bit of an attitude. "I still like you; that hasn't changed. Some things, like that, you can't change. You don't know how hard I've tried not to like you, but you have all the qualities I admire in a man."

"What are those qualities? You like me because I'm nasty," he kidded.

"Yeah, that's one reason," I kidded right back, even though I was very serious.

"Seriously, you are real. You are direct. You don't hold back or bite your tongue. You know how to treat a woman and still maintain your position as the man in the relationship. I like that. I like take-charge men, probably because I've never had anyone to take care of me. I've always had to do everything for myself, so it's refreshing to lean on someone else."

"Well, that's how I was raised by my mama. To be a man. To be a provider, protector and lover."

"Your mama did a good job."

"Yeah, she did, seeing how difficult it is for a woman to raise a boy into a man. What she missed, I picked up from the streets; that's why I'm a little rough around the edges."

"I like your rough edges. Does she live in Houston?"

"No. She is happily married and happily retired, living in Phoenix. The weather there does wonders for her severe asthma, and she is finally taking care of herself, as opposed to her taking care of someone else. We usually talk at least once a week."

I nodded and smiled.

"I wish other men had your upbringing," I said in a near whisper. "There were so many times I needed a protector."

"You must have been dealing with some real knuckleheads."

"You can say that. Some men wanted to take advantage of my kindness, but they soon learned."

"How did they learn? Educate me."

"I cut their dicks off and stuffed it in their big, fat, dominating mouths."

Xavier didn't say a single word. Then I burst into uncontrollable giggles.

"I had you going, didn't I?"

"Yeah. You are one crazy chick. I've never been to your spot. Why don't I roll by?" he said smoothly.

"It's almost one o'clock in the morning."

"The night is still young," he stated. "It's Friday night."

"No, it's late and I'm already dressed for bed."

I could tell he didn't expect that answer. In fact, I didn't expect to say that either. I surprised myself. I knew his little girlfriend had left town for a few days, because I'd watched her load her suitcase and overnight bag and drive off.

While the cat was away, the dog wanted to play. Not tonight. I wasn't going to make it that easy, no matter how badly I wanted that man. I craved to feel his hands roaming over my body, his tongue deep inside me. Yet, I couldn't give in.

"We don't have to go anywhere. We can hang out at your place."

"I don't think so, not tonight anyway. I'll give you a raincheck, babe."

"Okay. If that's how you want it." I could hear the disappointment clearly etched in his tone.

"Cool."

"You said you were ready for bed. What are you wearing?"

"Why?" I asked.

"I'm curious. Are you wearing something sexy?"

"Depends on what you consider sexy. I have on a holey T-shirt and some white grandmama panties."

"Sounds sexy to me."

I laughed as only Xavier could make me laugh. "You are too stupid. How can an old tee and grandma panties sound sexy?"

"Anything is sexy on you, Pilar. I bet your dark nipples are poking through the shirt as we speak."

I didn't respond. I simply swallowed the thick lump in my throat.

"I love when they get erect and stand out for me like two thick blackberries waiting to be plucked."

I swallowed again and changed position on the sofa.

"I bet you are wet now," he whispered.

"Maybe."

"I know you are. Whenever I talk nasty to you, it always turns you on. Makes you hot."

Xavier was right. I was starting to toss and turn on the sofa. The heat was already rising from between my thighs as I imagined his fingers inside me doing their magical dance of lust.

"Don't you wish I was there, touching you the way you like to be touched?" he asked seductively. "I know exactly what turns you on."

"How would you touch me?" I asked.

"I'd spread you wide and gently place my mouth on your clit and suck you until you came in my mouth."

"You are so nasty."

"And you love it."

"Where's Kendall tonight?" I asked, totally off the subject at hand.

"Keep her out of this."

"Why? You remind me every chance you get that you have a future wifey-to-be. One who is absolutely perfect, unlike me. I was just curious as to where she was."

"I don't get you, Pilar. One minute you are hot and the next cold. It's like you have two personalities. What's up with that? Next time, warn me when your other personality is going to show up so I can fucking leave. That shit came totally out of left field."

"Did it? Did it really? You talk all that dirty shit to me, fuck me any way you want to and then in another breath tell me about the wonderful fiancée that you have. I don't get you. What's up with that?"

"Like I said before, Pilar, keep Kendall out of this. This is between you and me."

"Make me, Xavier," I screamed. "Make me! I dare you!"

"Pilar, you are a piece of work, but I'm not going to go there with you."

"Whatever! Why aren't you saying these things to her at one o'clock in the morning? Why don't you fuck her? Oops, I forgot; you make love to her, right? My bad."

"You know what? You are one crazy bitch, literally. One minute you are slobbering all over my dick, and the next you really do act like you want to cut it off. I don't get you at all."

"That's the problem! You don't get me! You only want what's between my legs! You could care less about anything else I have to offer. You say what I want to hear, send me all these mixed messages, fuck with my mind, get what you want, and then I'm simply tossed away."

"Let me go. This was a mistake. A huge one," he said.

"Oh, you can't handle the truth now? Look at baby boy run. Go ahead. I'm not stopping you. Go! Run home to Mommy so you can suck on her tit some more."

"Baby, I can handle it. Believe that. You just don't see the truth. Only your distorted version. Pilar, you live in lala land. Pull your head out of the sand."

"Can't you see that we are so much alike? Why can't you see that? Open your eyes. We complement each other. From our creativity, to our passion, to our aggressiveness, to simply loving to satisfy our carnal desires. Can't you see that? We are like yin and yang. I could be so good for you."

"All I see is that I shouldn't have called. You are too much damn drama for me, Pilar. I think you thrive on that shit. You are not bringing that into my life. I'm not going there with you. Not now. Not ever. Do you understand?"

"Oh, I understand perfectly, more than you think."

There was a silent pause.

"You know what? You were a huge mistake."

"No, it was a mistake after you didn't get your way. I didn't eagerly invite you over for a late night booty call, so you could climb on top of me and grind for hours so that I could barely walk the next day and then you make it home in time for wifey. So sorry to disappoint you!"

"You don't have to worry about me calling your crazy ass again. That's a bet. Don't send me any more of those pathetic e-mails either."

"They can't be as pathetic as your non-fucking fiancée."

"Pilar, I've warned you to stop talking about . . ."

"Make me, Xavier. Make me stop talking about her. You can't tell me to jump and expect me to ask how high. I'm not the one."

"Keep her name out of your mouth."

"Or what, Xavier? What are you going to do about it?"

Silence.

"That's what I thought. Nothing. I'm not one of your groupies on the road. You can't dismiss me like I'm invisible!"

"Bitch, you are no different than—"

"You have one more time to call me a bitch. You don't have

to love me, you don't even have to like me, but you will respect me."

"Like I said, bitch—"

"I'm no longer listening, so talk to this," I screamed and ended the call, slamming my phone repeatedly on the arm of the sofa. "You will regret that, Xavier. I guarantee it," I said into the stillness of my apartment.

Why was it so hard for this man to love me? For the life of me, I couldn't understand it. I gave him my all and he treated me like nothing. Couldn't he see just how much I cherished the ground he walked on? He was always hurting me when all I wanted was to love him.

Who the hell was he calling crazy and a bitch? I had been patient with Xavier, but my patience was quickly running thin. If he wanted to see crazy, I could show him crazy. That was easy.

Chapter 24

XAVIER

All that glitters isn't gold.

What was I thinking? Thinking with the wrong head again. What in the hell is wrong with me? Dré had warned me. Everything I knew instinctively was warning me, and I still went and called her up. Stupid. Was I really willing to lose everything for some ass?

In the past, I had joked about Pilar being a little off, but I now knew without a shadow of a doubt the woman was definitely psycho. All that shit about us being meant for each other, soul mates. Was she from another planet? Did the Martians land and drop her off? At first, I thought she was joking, but now, I think she believed all that shit. She was definitely living in her own little world. Psycho.

Sunday, I lounged around my house all day. Didn't do a damn thing. I had talked to my baby Kendall earlier that morning and she appeared mellow, nice and relaxed. Going home did her good. She surprised me by telling me how much she wanted me and couldn't wait to get home to prove it. That made my day. I worked hard Monday through Friday, so I enjoyed my weekends doing whatever I wanted to do, no commitments. I watched a couple of movies I had been meaning to check out, worked out like a crazy man in my home gym and enjoyed the luxury of walking around in my drawers, unshaven. Heaven.

On the weekends, I typically didn't check my e-mail because the way I saw it, whatever someone wanted with me could wait until Monday morning. If my agent or editor needed me, they knew my digits and how to reach me. I was in for a big surprise when I logged on bright and early Monday morning. I literally had over one hundred e-mails from Psycho Pilar. I read a few and simply deleted the others, shaking my head. I didn't know if I should pity her or hire a fulltime bodyguard.

Xavier. Babe. I'm sooo sorry. Will you forgive me? Please? I don't know what came over me. I've been under so much stress with the move to Houston, my new project and everything else that is going on in my life. I didn't mean anything I said. If I could take it back, I would.

Hey, babe. Did you get my last e-mail? Please answer me. I hate it when you are mad at me. I didn't mean one word of what I said Friday night. Not a word.

Xavier, it kills me when you treat me like I'm invisible. Makes me feel like shit. Talk to me. Chat back. Please. Just acknowledge me. Say that you forgive me. Scream at me. Say something. That's all I ask.

I know you've been online because I saw where you logged into your MySpace page. Why are you treating me like this?

Babe. Why don't we meet somewhere? You wanted to come by the other night, so let's meet up. You know we always have fun when we're together. I'm sitting here, right now, imagining your big, black, juicy dick buried deep inside my quivering pussy. Don't you want some? It's yours for the taking. You can have as much as you'd like. Do whatever you like.

Xavier, don't answer back then. You spineless bitch. I hate your ass! I hate your ass so much right about now! You get a sick pleasure out of hurting me. Playing games with my mind. You spineless bitch motherfucker. You will be sorry. I guarantee it. You can't ignore me forever.

I'm sorry, babe. I didn't mean to say that. You just bring out the worst in me. When you hurt me, I lash out. It's just in me, the way I was raised. You are the only man that makes me feel special, at least when it's just you and me behind closed doors. Then, I have your undivided attention and I know you see me. I want you to see me.

Most of the time, I don't feel special. When I was growing up, mostly I was in the way, a burden. At least, that's how I felt. That's what I was told. I don't want to just be in your way. Visible only when you want to use me. I like you. I like you so much. Why can't you like me back? You say you do, but your actions speak otherwise. Why? Am I that bad of a person?

Xavier? Xavier? Xavier? You know I'd do anything for you, just to be in your presence, just to feel your touch. I'd even take a back seat and just be your mistress if that would make you happy. I think you are wonderful, a wonderful writer, a wonderful person, a wonderful lover. I like you. I let you screw me and take us both to heaven. Isn't that enough? Why isn't that enough? What am I doing wrong?

Babe, please talk to me! Please. I need you to acknowledge me. Please. Acknowledge me.

If you don't talk to me, I'm going to do something really bad to myself, and I want you to live the rest of your life knowing you caused me to hurt myself. I'll leave a note and tell the world what a lousy, no good, self-serving coward you are. Coward because you can't face the truth. Can you live with that? You probably can because you don't care about anyone but your damn self-absorbed self. The sun doesn't rise and set around you.

I HATE YOU!!! I HATE YOU!!!

Xavier, please talk to me. I'm lost without you. My soul feels so empty without you. I miss you, Pilar.

After I read some of Pilar's e-mails, I didn't know what to think or what to do. I shook my head in utter amazement; I honestly couldn't believe it. The e-mails went on and on; I deleted over one hundred of them. I admit, Pilar had gotten to me by throwing me off balance. She shook me up. I was angry, fed up with her dramatics and surprisingly to me, I was a little scared. The hairs on the back of my neck were literally standing up. I realized it was best to keep my distance going forward. However, I'd soon learn that would be easier said than done.

Chapter 25

PILAR

Forgive and forget.

I had forgiven Xavier. Maybe I hadn't forgotten, but I can honestly say I had forgiven. I realized I started our argument out of my own insecurities. It was mostly my fault, but I did have to pass some of the blame his way. He hadn't responded to any of my e-mails and the last few times I tried to call him, he hung up on me. I wasn't worried. I knew it was just a matter of time before he forgave me and things returned to normal. Normal for us, anyway, because normal is a relative term. I sensed it was only a matter of time before he realized we were meant for each other. I had all the time in the world. I was very patient.

I walked slowly from room to room, checking out everything . . . even the bathrooms and closets. I didn't want to miss anything. I wanted to see, feel and experience all there was to see, feel and experience. I leisurely strolled around in awe as if I were in a museum, reveling in history and the remarkable accomplishments of mankind. My head was spinning because there was so much to take in. My head was moving left, right, up and down, as my eager eyes took in my surroundings.

I lovingly ran the palm of my hand over the spit-polished banister that led upstairs to the upper level. My bare feet sank into the thick plush carpet, and it felt like I was walking on billowy clouds.

Xavier had exquisite taste. He chose bold and daring color combinations that I would pick if I were decorating a home. When I eventually moved in with him, which I would, there wouldn't be much to change in the décor because we shared such similar tastes. Just one more reason I knew we were made for each other.

I finally made my way into the master bedroom. This was the room I had been dying to check out since I stepped in the front door. It was huge and spacious. It was definitely Xavier; had his name written all over it. His personality and aura were all over that room because every inch reeked of him. Of course, the centerpiece of the bedroom was the massive oak bed that sat smack in the middle of the bedroom in all its glory, with thick columns that nearly touched the ceiling. *If walls could talk.* Xavier was a big man, so this bed was perfect for him.

I gently ran my fingers over the black comforter and lay down, imaging myself lying there next to Xavier as he held me in his strong arms and told me how much he loved me. How we were meant to be together forever. How he loved me since the first time he saw me. I rolled around and just laughed at the sheer joy of being in his space. I couldn't believe I was here. This was where I belonged.

It hadn't been hard to get into Xavier's house. I had made an imprint of his key the last time we were together. Of course, he was none the wiser. It was amazing what could be done in only a matter of a few seconds. After that, it was as simple as getting someone to make a key for me, for the right price. I'd found everyone had a price.

I wandered out of his bedroom and roamed around, checking out his upstairs office. Xavier was extremely neat. Everything was in its proper place, much like his women. However, I wasn't surprised at his neatness because whenever we had been together, I'd toss my clothes to the floor and he'd always pick them up, fold them neatly and place them on a chair.

Xavier's computer was state of the art. I figured this was where he typed out his masterpieces. I sat down in the huge leather swivel chair and imagined him typing away each and every day, creating characters that would forever live on, long after he was dead and gone. He was so creative and smart and sexy.

Xavier had an extensive hardcover book and movie collection. I scanned through a few of the titles. I saw all the first print editions of his previous titles. His taste in literature was literally across the board with eclectic tastes. He read everything from contemporary fiction, to classics, to science fiction, to erotica to non-fiction to autobiographies to African-American history.

In his bathroom was a huge Jacuzzi tub that at least four people could easily fit in. I imagined the two of us sipping glasses of wine and chilling there. I shuffled through his toiletries to find out what products he preferred. I even checked out his toothbrush, ran my fingers across the firm bristles and used it to brush my teeth. Opened the medicine cabinet and looked through his prescriptions.

Xavier had a lovely home. He didn't disappoint. I checked out every minute detail. In the kitchen pantry, I even looked through his canned products, all neatly lined up, to see what he enjoyed eating, and made a mental note. Around lunchtime, I fixed myself a sandwich in the kitchen, at his island. I went to the refrigerator and pulled out bread, turkey slices, crispy lettuce, red ripe tomatoes and a crunchy pickle on the side. I made myself a turkey sandwich on wheat. Then I sat down at the dining table and ate, looking peacefully out the huge bay window that overlooked his expansive back yard. I washed my meal down with some Perrier water from the stainless steel refrigerator. It was so peaceful and quiet there. I could stay there forever. It was my secret haven. A secret, perfect paradise.

After I cleaned up, making sure I wiped up every crumb, I slowly walked back upstairs. I wasn't concerned with the time because I knew Xavier was at Starbucks, writing. I'd followed him there earlier and watched him walk in with his laptop bag thrown across his shoulder. Based on previous history, I knew he'd be there for a while, lost in his fictional characters and imaginary world.

I casually strolled back into the master bedroom and eagerly pulled off my socks and warm up pants, shirt, panties and bra. I reclined on his bed totally nude. I got back up to get under the clean fresh, sheets. I inhaled and could clearly smell the masculine scent of Xavier. I knew his smell well. Had memorized his unique aroma. I inhaled again and pulled the sheet closer to me.

I opened my legs, closed my eyes and pictured Xavier in my mind. Tall, dark and handsome. I slowly masturbated, eased my fingers inside my womanhood and slowly stroked. I came two times in his bed, leaving my mark. Marking my territory. Afterward, I redressed, minus my black, lacy panties. Those I slid underneath his mattress for safekeeping. I made up the bed; double-checked to make sure everything was as I had found it and strolled downstairs. After putting on my shoes, I quietly slipped out the front door, just as quietly as I'd slipped in.

Xavier would come home an hour later and be none the wiser.

Chapter 26

XAVIER

Houston, there is a problem.

I replayed the voice mail over and then again. I had listened to it three times already. Tried to get a sense if she was messing with me. The words I heard were like beacons of joy to my ears. *I'm leaving. I'm leaving Houston.*

I literally wanted to jump for joy. Wanted to do the happy dance. I think I did pump my fist a couple of times into the air. Pilar was leaving Houston. She had just made me the happiest man in Texas. No more psycho bitch breathing the same air that I breathed.

There was one catch. There's always a catch. She wanted to meet with me. Say her final goodbyes before she left. According to her, she wanted to make sure we didn't end our *friendship* on bad terms. What friendship? If we were friends, then I definitely didn't need any enemies. At this point, if it was going to speed up her moving out of Houston and out of my life, I was willing to do almost anything. Even if it meant meeting with her.

* * *

Even though every fiber in my body was screaming no, run, telling me I was going to regret it, I reluctantly agreed to meet and talk with Pilar. It was Thursday evening as I found myself driving to a local barbecue restaurant I had recommended. One, the food was delicious and two, there would be lots of people there. If Pilar was going to freak out, at least it would be in a public place.

My phone rang and I viewed the caller ID. I regretted the day I phoned her and she captured my number. Big mistake.

"Hello."

"Hi," I heard Pilar's voice shyly say.

"Talk," I said somewhat coldly.

"I just wanted to make sure you were still coming."

"Damn, I said I was coming, didn't I?"

"Yes, I know. I just wanted to make sure you didn't change your mind at the last minute and I'm left sitting here and you be a no show."

"I'll be there in five minutes," I said and I hung up.

I was prepared to try my very best to make it through this dinner if it meant getting Pilar out of my life, once and forever. I pulled into the parking lot of the restaurant that was known for serving some of the best barbecue in Texas. For this time of the evening, I was surprised that the parking lot was not packed to capacity. I wanted lots and lots of people around us. However, I easily found a parking space near the entrance.

I took a deep breath, stepped out of my car and pressed the keypad to lock it. It was now or never. Once I walked into the restaurant, I looked around, trying to locate Pilar. She wasn't hard to find. She was the most beautiful woman in the room, sitting in a corner booth looking totally stunning. She waved shyly to get my attention. I slowly walked over, not sure what to expect or which Pilar would be waiting.

I checked her out as I headed her way. Pilar looked like she had recently gotten her hair done; every strand was in place and her makeup was flawless. She had on a form-fitting black dress that dipped low in the front and matching heels. It was casually elegant. I made it to the table and reluctantly sat down across from her.

"Hi."

"Hi."

"Thanks for coming."

I nodded.

"I realize this must have been very difficult for you, agreeing to meet me, but I wanted to make sure we were okay with each other before I left town."

"I don't think this was necessary, but I'm here now. I can't stay long, so let's make this quick."

"I understand," she said softly.

I sat across from her and watched her study the menu like she was studying for a math test. There was such a sadness in her doe-like eyes. I almost felt sorry for her. Almost.

Pilar looked up and smiled, but the smile never quite reached her eyes. Her eyes were empty. Hollow. "Do you suggest anything from the menu?"

"You'll be safe ordering anything. The barbeque is off the chain. If you know anything about Texas, then you know Texas is known for its barbeque. Best in the country."

"Cool. I'm so glad you could come, Xavier. I mean that and appreciate this. I would hate to leave thinking you hate me. I know you have every right to . . ."

"I don't hate you, Pilar. I do think you have some issues you need to deal with. Some of your actions have been extreme. That's putting it mildly."

She didn't say anything, just looked down and studied the menu even more. I don't think she appreciated my comment, but the way I saw it, the truth will set you free.

"I didn't mean to upset you, Pilar, but it's not normal to obsess over a person like you do."

"I'm not obsessed with you, Xavier."

"Pilar, yes, you are!"

"No, I'm not."

"Okay, suit yourself."

"If I'm such a horrible person, why do you keep coming back?"

I opened my mouth to speak, then closed it. There was an awkward moment of silence. Truthfully, I couldn't answer that question. It wasn't just the pussy. It was good, but I could get that anywhere. Why did I keep coming back? What did that say about me as a man?

"Excuse me. I have to go to the restroom," she said, abruptly grabbing her large black tote and hurrying away.

I watched her walk away and saw a few male heads turn in her direction. If only they knew how damn crazy she was. Straight looney tunes. However, I must admit she was wearing that dress. I thought, so far so good.

When Pilar came back, her eyes appeared to be red and puffy. Like she had been crying.

"Are you okay?" I asked, lightly touching her arm.

She nodded, jerked her arm away like I had burnt her and sat down.

"The waitress came by when you were in the restroom, so I went ahead and placed our meal and drink orders."

"That's fine. I trust your judgment. I'm sure you chose something I'll enjoy," she said, clearing her throat several times.

"By the way, you look very nice tonight," I said.

"Thank you," she said, not making eye contact.

"Pilar?"

"Yes."

"Please look at me."

"Okay."

She slowly looked up, never really connecting with me.

"Pilar, if it means anything, I didn't mean to hurt you or lead you on in any way. I really thought I was upfront about my situation, and I really thought that was understood from the very beginning. Honestly, I don't feel I lied to you or misled you."

"Shhh," she said, placing her fingers on my lips. "Let's just enjoy our last meal together. It doesn't matter now. Does it?"

"I guess not."

If that was how she wanted tonight to play out, fine with me. I could act like all was cool with us. I could do almost anything as long as I knew she was getting the hell out of Texas. Out of my life.

As dinner progressed, I think Pilar had actually convinced herself that nothing had happened between us. I think she totally placed out of her mind the angry, hurtful words we had exchanged. Words that could never be taken back. I started to think maybe I had imagined it myself. Because, believe it or not, we were having a good time.

Much like the last time, I had to admit, I did enjoy talking to Pilar and hanging out with her. She wasn't one of those self-absorbed females. She enjoyed hearing my opinions and thoughts on various topics. I don't know a man alive who didn't like to hear himself talk and have a beautiful woman hang on to his every word.

"When is your next book coming out?" she asked. "I can't wait too long."

"First of next year."

"That's right. Will you autograph a copy for me?"

"Of course I will," I lied. After today, I prayed I'd never set eyes on Pilar again, not even in my next life.

There was a silence. Something changed; Pilar's body language was different. Her demeanor was no longer icy cold.

"Come here. You have sauce on your cheek. Right there," she said, pointing to her own cheek.

"I'll get it, " I said, reaching for my napkin and wiping.

"No. You didn't get it all. Come here. Lean over. I don't bite." She laughed at that.

I reluctantly leaned over and Pilar wiped the sauce off my cheek with her middle finger and then proceeded to suck it off her finger, real slow and sensual. She smiled and made eye contact.

That simple gesture sent shivers up and down my spine.

She smiled sweetly. She had such an angelic, sweet face.

"I bet female book club members love you."

"What do you mean by that?" I asked, reclining in my seat.

"You know what I mean. I bet you have women propositioning you left and right."

"Maybe."

"Maybe? Please. I saw how those women were all over you in Atlanta. Those book club groupies love a fine, sexy, tall, dark and handsome male author. In fact, I bet other female authors try to get a taste too."

"If they do, that doesn't mean I have to act on it."

"Sure."

"What is that supposed to mean?"

"Be for real, Xavier. As much as you love women, you mean to tell me you have never, ever slept with anyone? One of your book club readers or fellow female authors, while you were on the road touring?"

"I'm not saying I'm perfect. We both know I'm not. I've had a few indiscretions, but don't sit there and act like I'll screw anything female that walks and talks and reads one of my books."

Pilar simply stared at me and didn't say anything.

"What?"

"I was just thinking how I pity your future wife. I could never be married to a man like you; I could never trust you. You will be one of those married bachelors. I don't think you could ever fully commit yourself to anyone for very long because once the challenge is gone, you lose interest. You have too much fun with the chase. I'd always wonder if you were screwing someone while you were on the road," Pilar said, very matter-of-factly.

You are entitled to your opinion no matter how wrong it may be," I stated as calmly as possible. "Everybody has one."

"You break my heart, Xavier."

I didn't say anything, simply waited for her to finish.

"You can't recognize love when it is staring you dead in the face. Why me?" she asked.

"Excuse me?"

"Why me? Why did you hook up with me?"

"Because you are a beautiful, intelligent woman, Pilar. You don't seem to realize just how sexy you are. You piqued my interest and I wanted to get to know you better."

That brought the first genuine smile of the night.

Pilar reached for my hand and I didn't pull away. "Things could have been so different if I had met you years ago."

"Maybe. Damn, who knows? In another day and time. Who knows? I don't live by woulda, coulda, shoulda."

"If I had met you years ago, you probably wouldn't have even liked me," she said. "I was another person then. Not as confident in who and what I am today."

"You are probably right. Who knows? We can't rewrite the past."

"No, we can't. We were destined to meet at this moment in time—at this stage in our lives. The universe always places us exactly where we need to be," she said.

I kind of mumbled something, nodded my head and took a sip of water.

Pilar looked me dead in the eyes and spoke slowly. "I want you. I want you so bad. I need you and you don't even realize it." And when I looked at her, I knew she really did. I could feel her passion. Her craving. Her longing. She was literally trembling. I could almost see the heat rising from her body.

"When you haven't touched me in days, I start to have withdrawal symptoms."

"Pilar, I don't think—"

"I want to be with you one last time. That's all. One more

time and then I can walk away. Is that asking for too much?" The look in her eyes pleaded with me to touch her one more time.

I pulled my hand away. "Pilar, as much as I desire you, I don't think that would be a good idea."

"But—"

"I think we should leave it like it is, two friends having a fun dinner and call it a night."

"If you say so," she said, looking back down at the table and retreating inward again.

Our waiter had perfect timing. He chose that moment to walk back over with the check. I sent a silent thank you up to heaven.

"I have to go to the restroom again," Pilar said in a pitiful voice.

"Go ahead. I'll pay the check and meet you up front."

She got up, carrying her big black tote, and headed off to the restroom.

I settled the check and waited and waited. Pilar still hadn't made it back to our table or to the front of the restaurant. I stood up and walked near the back where the restrooms were located. Just as I neared the women's restroom, she came out. She hadn't seen me yet. She was sniffling and trying to compose herself.

"Thought you had gotten lost in there," I said, gesturing toward the restroom door.

"You scared me," she said, almost falling against the wall.

I grabbed her arm to steady her. "You okay?"

When I touched her, I swear, a bolt of electricity shot through me. Charged up from the tip of my fingers to the top of my arm. We locked eyes. If she felt it, she didn't say anything.

I couldn't resist. All resistance drained out of me in an instant. I did something I had wanted to do all evening.

I bent down and kissed her. Kissed her softly at first, slow and sweet, and then more passionately, savoring her. I wrapped my arms around her, holding her tight against my body. Her body was burning up. We fell against the wall, locked in an embrace. She offered me her tongue and I took it, eagerly accepted it into my mouth. We were locked in desire.

"What do you do to me? I can't get enough of you," I moaned as she squeezed my tool through my pants. "As mad as you make me, I still can't get enough."

"I want you. One last time. I want to feel you slide deep inside me and open me up. Just one time, that's all I'm asking for."

Pilar had me so hot and bothered I couldn't think straight.

My hands roamed up and down her body, remembering familiar crevices and curves. I don't know what came over me. Still feeling her up, I led her into the women's restroom.

After checking to make sure no one was in there, I quickly locked the door and went back to kissing her, her eyes, nose and neck. She moaned and leaned hungrily into me, merging her body with mine. Two became one. I quickly turned her around, face against the wall, and pulled up her dress in one swift movement.

"Is this what you want?" I asked, pulling my dick out of my unzipped pants and rubbing it against her ass cheeks.

"Yes," she moaned again, reaching around to touch it. "Yes."

"I'm going to give it to you. One for the road. Something to remember me by," I whispered into her ear. She shivered violently against my touch.

I eased myself inside, after checking her wetness with two fingers. This time, I let out a loud moan. She was so hot and wet. Her walls literally collapsed around my dick, sucking it in like a vacuum. My knees became weak; I leaned on her to support myself.

"Hmmm, you feel so damn good."

She turned her face around and stuck her tongue back in my mouth. I started moving in and out of her, slowly at first. Savored the intense pleasure. Embraced her softness. Her passion and vulnerability. If I were honest with myself, I'd admit that her weakness for me empowered me. I knew she'd do anything for me. I drew strength from her weakness.

"Damn. You make me so hard."

"Do I, babe?"

"You like this?" I asked, pumping in and out. With each inward grind, she'd hit against the wall.

"Yes, babe. Take all you want. This is all yours," she moaned, barely audible, again and again.

At this point, we had moved over to the sinks. I had her bend over, holding on to the sink with both hands, as I went in and out of her at a frantic, urgent pace. She had her eyes closed, head thrown back and was taking all of me. The restroom echoed with the wet, slapping sound of my dick meeting her pussy, up to the hilt.

"Pull the top of your dress down and play with your nipples."

She kept moaning. Didn't pay me any attention.

"Pilar, play with your nipples. I want to watch."

She obliged. As I screwed her from behind, in the mirror I watched her tweak her nipples and saw the wave of ecstasy pass over her face, contorting her features to what almost looked like pain. I was close to coming. I wanted to get her off first, but it was hard to hold back.

"Turn around," I said, roughly swinging her around by the arm.

As she half reclined on the sink, I held her leg up with my hand and entered her again.

"Tell me to fuck you. Beg for this big dick to go up inside you."

"Fuck me, babe."

"Oh, yeah."

"Harder! Deeper!"

"Ohhh, baby. Tell me what you want."

"Give it to me! Give it all to me! Yes, give it to me!" she chanted.

Then, I made the mistake of a lifetime. Looking back, I realize that was the comment that made the shit truly hit the fan. One comment took our abnormal relationship to another level entirely.

"Oh, Kendall, baby."

Just as I was coming, I called her, Kendall. *Shit.*

She stopped. Stopped moving. Tried to pull my dick out of her just as I was coming and coming hard. I pulled her close, pulled her face to my chest and held her tight against her constant, violent struggles to get me out of her. As she hit me, slapped against my shoulder, clawed at my face, I grabbed her leg, held on tight and came. Call me a dog, but there was no way that I was not going to get that nut. I'm sorry, but it was feeling too good to stop.

"What did you call me?" she asked, staring me down with venom in her eyes, breathing hard and raspy as I released my grip.

"What are you talking about?" I asked between breaths, halfway collapsed on the sink.

"I know you didn't just call me Kendall!"

"You are hearing things," I said, dismissing her comments away as if they were false.

She didn't comment, simply looked into my face for an ounce of truth.

"Are you paranoid or something? I know the difference. There's no way I'd confuse the two of you."

Pilar stared at me coldly. If looks could kill, I would have been dead on the spot.

"Let's go check into a hotel for a few hours. I still don't have my fill of you," I said. "You have some good pussy, girl. I could just live in it."

Pilar smiled sweetly. "Okay, sounds good."

My breathing had finally returned to normal.

"Lead the way."

She unlocked the door and did just that. Led the way. And I followed like a lamb to slaughter.

If I had been paying close attention, I would have noticed that the smile never reached her eyes. In fact, another much more dangerous emotion was present and accompanied us straight to the hotel.

Chapter 27

PILAR

The psycho has entered the building.

This time, I trailed Xavier to a nearby hotel. I needed my car and didn't want to have to rely on him to take me back or vice versa when we were finished. I wanted to make a quick, hasty exit.

The entire drive over, I secretly fumed inside. How dare he? How dare he? The nerve of him. That arrogant, self-serving bastard. He came inside me, but had the audacity to call me another female's name. Oh, hell no! At least give me the credit for taking him there and getting him off. And then, he tried to lie about it. Xavier is not a good liar. At least not to someone like me, experienced in sniffing out the bullshit. He was knee deep in his.

It was at that moment I realized what I had to do. I suddenly knew I had to take drastic measures to make him hear, see and understand me. Understand in no uncertain terms that I meant business. Xavier was going to take me seriously once and for all. What I had been doing earlier was child's play. Now the real game was about to begin. If he didn't know, he'd better learn. He'd soon find out that I played to win.

I glanced over at the black tote that sat in the passenger seat next to me. Yeah, I was going to show his ass that you didn't mess with Pilar. Don't call me no weak-ass, bookwormish, non-fucking Kendall. When it was all said and done, he would never forget my name. Yeah, I was going to show him exactly what I was made of. Just like I had shown the others. I'm patient, but you can only push me so far before I pushed back. Well, I was ready to push back. And I took no prisoners.

Roughly ten minutes later, I pulled in beside Xavier and waited for him to come around and open my car door. We walked hand in hand the short distance inside. I sat quietly in the lobby as he registered, checking out the beautiful décor. Pastel, muted colors along with framed prints were the perfect blend, paired with the live plants and flowers that were in every nook and cranny. One distinct thing I liked about Xavier was that he had class and appreciated the finer things in life. He always took me to the best hotels for our little rendezvous.

As Xavier and I rode up in the elevator, I was now simmering again. I visualized myself as a teapot slowly starting to brew until it blew its lid. Xavier couldn't tell because he was all over me, feeling me up. I smiled sweetly and let him have his fun. I would have mine soon enough.

The elevator door finally opened on our floor and we got off to find our corner room. He always wanted the corner room for some unknown reason. Anyone who noticed us would have thought we were a typical, average loving couple. They had no clue as to the fury I tried to contain.

Xavier opened the door with the key card and gestured for me to enter. We didn't even bother to turn on any lights. I dropped my tote by the door as Xavier came up behind me and nibbled on my ear. I teasingly pushed him away.

"Hey, babe. Why don't you order some wine? Let's not rush our time together."

"Sounds good. Go ahead and make yourself comfortable and I'll call room service," he said.

"Do you care for any particular brand?" he asked.

"No. I trust your judgment completely. Order whatever you would like."

I walked into the bathroom to freshen up. I could hear Xavier as he placed our order and moved around the room. When I came out of the bathroom donning a fluffy white robe provided by the hotel, the drapes had been opened to reveal a stunning view of the city. Xavier had soft, romantic music playing in the background from his MP3 player and the mood was set. He smiled at me. He was such a charming bastard.

As I walked by to sit in the chair nearest the bed, he reached for my hand, lovingly.

"What's wrong?" he said, like he was concerned. Yeah, he was concerned I was going to change my mind and not give him any. That was as far as his concern went.

"Nothing, babe. I'm just a little tired, that's all. It's been a long day."

"You sure? You've been acting different since we left the restaurant."

"Have I?" I asked.

"Don't answer a question with a question."

"I haven't noticed. I guess I can't believe this is our last night together."

"Well, let's just enjoy it and each other," he stated, sitting on the ottoman in front of my chair. He didn't have on anything other than a pair of dark boxers. I could never get enough of looking at his sculpted body. The man was fine. Too fine for his own good.

"Will you miss me?" I asked, looking anxiously at him.

"Pilar?"

"I mean, just a little?"

"Pilar, please don't start."

He slowly opened up my robe and pulled it off my shoulders. Underneath, I had on a red bra and thong panties.

"Beautiful. Simply beautiful."

Xavier ran his hand down my neck and pushed up my bra to expose my breasts. They literally tumbled out for him.

"Lovely."

He gently licked and nibbled a trail from my breasts to my stomach to my womanhood. My nipples instantly perked up. When he reached the spot between my legs, he blew his hot breath through the sheer fabric of my thong. Then blew again. Goosebumps popped up on my arms. Involuntarily, my body responded by arching my back and opening my legs wider to give him easier access.

He pulled the flimsy fabric of my thong aside and gently rubbed on my clit with his thumb. I moaned softly, even though I didn't want to. I didn't want him to have the satisfaction of bringing me any pleasure. He already thought I was whipped. I didn't want to be just another notch on his belt.

Xavier leaned down and slowly and gently licked my clit with his tongue. Up and down. Up and down. Over and over. Used a finger to open me up even more, revealing my wetness. I pulled his head back in mid-lick.

"Well?"

"Well, what?" he moaned, with half-closed eyes.

"Will you miss me?"

Xavier didn't answer, simply bit down roughly on my nipple.

I yelped in pain.

"That hurt," I said. "Don't do that again."

"Be quiet then. Don't talk. Relax."

I opened my mouth to say something again.

"Shhh, what did I say? Didn't I tell you to be quiet?"

I started to protest him bossing me around.

"See, you are hardheaded. You're going to make me teach you a lesson."

To prove his point, he took both nipples in his fingers and twisted. It was a curious combination of pain and pleasure that I embraced.

"Stop," I cried, hitting at his hands.

He did it again.

"Oh, don't act like you don't like that S&M shit. You get all into that," he said, amused.

A few seconds later, there were a couple of light taps at the door. The mental image of Kendall walking in and catching us made me smile. I quickly covered up as Xavier went to open the door and pay for the wine. I was pissed that he wouldn't admit he'd miss me and that he had hurt me.

"Let me fix you a drink. Maybe that will relax you and then we can get back to pleasing one another," he said, opening the bottle.

I silently watched him pour two glasses of wine and bring one over to me. I took a couple of sips and enjoyed the sensation of the cool liquid easing down my throat.

"Aren't you drinking tonight?" I asked. His drink was still untouched, on the nightstand nearest the bed.

"I have to run to the bathroom first."

"Okay." I smiled. Perfect timing.

I only had a few minutes. I quickly jumped up as soon as the bathroom door closed. I retrieved the plastic vial from the pocket of my robe and quickly poured its liquid contents, GHB, or liquid ecstasy, as it was called on the streets, into Xavier's wine glass. Then I hurried back to my seat and sipped my own and waited for the fireworks to begin.

Xavier came out.

"Okay, where were we?" he asked, sitting back on the ottoman.

"Drink up," I said, pointing to his wine glass.

He reached for it and took a big gulp.

"Pull those off," he demanded, pointing to my thong. "Pull all that shit off."

I stood up and slid them to the floor as he watched. Then I discarded the robe and my bra. I never once took my eyes off him as I stood buck naked in front of him. He pulled me to him, wrapping his arm around my waist. My womanhood was pretty much in his face. He leaned in and breathed. He wet his finger with his mouth and stuck it deep inside me. I gasped. Then he began to eat me out—treated my stuff like it belonged to him and only him. I hated myself for loving it. I hated myself even more for still wanting him.

"Oh, babe," I moaned. "Let's move to the bed."

"Yes. Let's do that." He led me over to the king-size bed with his fingers still inside me.

"Don't forget your wine," I said.

He took a couple more gulps and his glass was empty. He placed it on the nightstand. Now, it was just a matter of time.

He lay on his back on the bed, with his hands resting behind his head, taking in my every move.

"What?" I asked.

"Nothing. I love watching you. Come over here and lay beside me."

I did as he requested and proceeded to lie down.

He then climbed above me and offered me his tool. I turned my head away.

"Quit playing, Pilar," he said, turning my head back to him with his hand.

"Open your mouth. Suck it. You know what turns me on."

I began to oblige.

"That's a good girl. That's right. Yesss, suck that shit."

Approximately fifteen minutes later, he was knocked out cold. I worked quickly and efficiently. I redressed in my bra and panties. I went over to the door and retrieved my black bag. My bag of goodies. It didn't take long to handcuff his wrists to the bedposts and tie his ankles up, good and tight, with cord.

He wasn't going anywhere until I said so. Now, I was running the show.

I straddled his chest and watched him breathe evenly for a few minutes. Such a handsome man. We could have been so happy together. He had to mess up everything—him and his precious Kendall. In that moment, I truly hated him.

I had everything that I'd need laid out. My clothes were neatly folded and placed on the chair at the table, just as he liked, and my keys were on top of the tote. I had already packed the wine glasses in my tote as well. I wouldn't want to leave anything behind to incriminate myself.

Showtime. I slapped the shit out of him. Once. Twice. Three times.

"Xavier! Xavier! Come out of it. Wake up!"

He slowly came to, looking disoriented and groggy. I was extra careful with the dosage of GHB that I administered. I didn't want him knocked out for longer than thirty minutes.

"Xavier! Look at me!" I screamed directly in his face.

I slapped him again.

He tried to sit up and realized he was bound. The expression on his face was priceless. I wished I had thought to video this so I could play it when I needed a good laugh.

"What the hell?"

"Shut up! You are going to listen to me for once!" I cried out. My hair was all in my flushed face, spilling forth in a cascade of uncontrollable spiral curls and I knew I looked like a wild, deranged woman.

"Pilar, if you don't untie me . . ." he said, twisting back and forth, struggling to free himself.

"You'll what, Xavier?"

"If you don't uncuff me, I'll—"

"You are not in a position to be telling me what to do," I said, tapping my finger, hard, into his chest with each word I uttered.

"I have the power now," I said, pinching one of his nipples. He grimaced.

"How does that feel? Doesn't feel so good, does it?"

I did it again, to the other nipple.

He yelped, much like I had done earlier.

"Oh, don't act like you don't like that S&M shit. You get all into that. Isn't that what you told me? What makes you think you can do anything you want with my body? This is my body."

"What? You are crazy."

"You are going to make me teach you a lesson."

"You are fucking crazy and when I get out of this, I'm going to beat your ass all over this room," he screamed.

"You think so?" I asked, taking out a mini black leather flogger whip.

"What are you going to do with that?" he said.

I hit him across the inner thigh. He screamed in pain.

"I can't hear you. Speak up, Xavier," I said, cupping my hand over my ear.

"Did you say I was crazy?" This time I hit him twice and I saw the welts form. I didn't want to break skin. Not yet anyway.

By now, he struggled to get out of the handcuffs and leg ties. However, he wasn't going anywhere until I let him.

I traced my finger around a nipple. I bent down and licked it.

"You know I loved you?" I was sobbing now. Snot was running down my nose and my mascara was running. I kept pushing my hair out of my face. "I loved you. Did you know that?"

I flogged him again, on the arm this time. "Answer me."

"Yes." The way his voice trembled and the way his jaw clenched and unclenched, I could tell it took everything in him to answer me.

"All I ever wanted was for you to love me back. But no, you only had eyes for Kendall. Pathetic, boring Kendall. I would have loved you so much better. Gave all of myself to you. Done anything for you. Can you say that about Kendall?"

I eased myself down to his balls. I thought his eyes were going to buck out of their sockets. I traced my finger around the two of them, picked up his tool and examined it like I was seeing it for the first time. I ran my hand up and down his shaft. Even in his terror, he expanded, grew in my palm.

"Do you think this makes you a man?" I asked. "Since you are not a man, maybe you don't need it."

"Please, Pilar, let me go. Don't take this any further. Let me go and I'll—we'll forget it ever happened."

I flogged him across the chest and he whimpered. "I'll let you go when I'm good and ready. You can't pull the strings all the time, Xavier. I can pull strings too. You think it's funny how you have me all confused and stressed out. Playing all these games with my mind. Sending mixed signals. One day acting like you are feeling me and the next acting like you can't tolerate my presence. A few words from you can make my day and when you don't talk to me, treat me like I'm invisible . . ."

"Pilar, untie me!"

"I just don't know . . . you confuse me. You make me crazy."

I played with his balls and I could feel Xavier's body stiffen from my touch. He got very still.

"What's wrong? You don't want me to touch you now? You can stick your fingers all up inside me, have me say nasty shit to you, but I can't touch you? You can stick your tongue inside me, but I can't touch you? You can make me suck your dick for an hour, but now, I can't touch you?"

I grabbed his balls and squeezed hard.

"You fucking bitch!" he screamed. "When I get my hands on you!"

"You are not going to do shit!" I sneered in his face, spittle flying. "Because if you do, I'll run to your precious Kendall and tell her everything. I'll tell her every single gory detail about her beloved, perfect Xavier. Are we on the same page?"

He nodded.

"I thought so."

I started to massage his dick with up and down, even, firm strokes. It slowly came to life again.

"I've always loved sucking your dick." I leaned down and rubbed it across my breasts and then ran my tongue around the tip, teased him, sucked him into my mouth inch by inch. I could tell he was trying his best not to enjoy it. However, a man's body will respond regardless.

"Come for me, Xavier," I cooed. "I want you to come in my mouth. I want to feel your seed going down my throat."

I had to give it to him. He tried his best not to come. However, I gave him the best blowjob ever. I was stroking and sucking and sucking and stroking and he couldn't hold back, not for long anyway. After he spewed his load into my mouth, I licked my lips.

"Hmmm. Sweet as honey."

I picked up his now limp tool and licked him clean. He couldn't do a damn thing but lie there, watch and enjoy.

"Does she do that?"

He turned his head away.

I snatched it back so he could see my face as I dug my nails into his cheeks and drew blood.

"One day you'll realize what you missed in me, babe."

I bent down to kiss him. He turned his head away again.

I flogged him again with the whip, this time on the other leg. He groaned in agony.

"Goodbye, Xavier," I said as I bent to kiss him. I inserted my tongue in his mouth and let him taste himself.

"I'll always love you. I've loved you since the first day I saw you. Actually, I've loved you since the first day I read your words and knew you were speaking to me. But you wouldn't know about love, would you?"

"Get me out of these!" he screamed, oblivious to my words.

"Shhh. Calm down. I'm going to get you out. Damn, give me time, man!"

I quickly pulled on my black dress, checked the room a second time to make sure I had everything. Wouldn't want to leave behind anything incriminating.

"What are you doing?" he asked, watching my every move.

"I'm leaving. Going back to Atlanta. Isn't that what you wanted?"

"Get me out of these," he screamed, struggling against the restraints.

I leaned down and stroked his cheek. "Remember what I told you. If you try to hurt me, I will sing like a canary to Kendall. Tell her all the nasty details."

I started picking up his clothing and packed them in my tote. I gathered up all the towels in the bathroom and packed them as well.

"What are you doing?"

"Don't worry; I'm going to let you go."

"What about my clothes?" he asked with panic written on his handsome face.

"Here's the deal: I'm going to take all your clothes with me to buy myself some time because I know when I let you out of those handcuffs you are going to want to hurt me, but I can't let that happen."

"You bitch," he screamed with venom spewing from his eyes.

"What's up with that foul language? Would you prefer I leave the handcuff key over there on the table?" I asked, walking over to the table in the far corner of the room. "Think you can reach it from the bed? I'm sure if you gave her a big tip, the maid would unlock the cuffs in the morning. Which way would you prefer?" I asked, with a big smile on my face, placing the key on the table.

He didn't respond. He simply turned his head to face the other wall.

"I can't hear you. Speak up or forever hold your peace," I screamed.

"Your way. I like the first way. You uncuff me."

"Cool. Say please with sugar on it."

"Please with sugar on it."

"Good boy," I said, stroking his bleeding cheek.

"So, I'm going to uncuff one hand and lay the key here on the bed beside you. You can uncuff your other hand and untie yourself after I'm gone. I think that's a fair deal."

"I can't believe this shit," he kept repeating, shaking his head from side to side. "I can't believe this shit."

"Oh, and you may want to have those cuts checked out by a doctor. Wouldn't want them to get infected. They look mighty nasty. Just a little something to remember me by."

"Fuck you!"

"I just did." I smiled sweetly.

"And Xavier, one more thing. In the future, be careful who you try to fuck with. Sometimes you get burnt."

He remained silent, but his eyes said it all. If he could have gotten loose, no doubt he would have fucked me up.

"Oh, I almost forgot," I said, reaching into my tote and pulling out my cell phone.

"Smile pretty for the camera. Say cheese." I took two photos on my camera phone. "This is for when I need a good laugh."

"You fucking bitch!" he spewed.

"That's Boss Bitch to you. And, you definitely enjoyed fucking this bitch. Nutted every time," I spat back.

He sneered.

"Any last words?"

Silence.

"I guess not. Okay, well, adios, Xavier. It's been real."

I walked over to the bed and whispered in his ear, "I'll miss you, babe. And I'll definitely miss that big black dick.

"Last question and you'd better get it right, Xavier, or I swear . . . What's my name?"

Xavier didn't respond quickly enough and I lifted my hand to strike him.

He whispered, "Pilar."

"I can't hear you," I said, slapping the side of his head.

"Pilar!" he screamed.

"Good boy. And don't you ever forget it. MY NAME IS PILAR!"

With that, I uncuffed his one hand and made sure I was out of his reach. Then, I left the key to the handcuff by his side. I was finished there. I calmly walked out the door and didn't look back. With my tote full of his clothes and shoes, Xavier wasn't going anywhere anytime soon. I did leave his cell phone, car keys and wallet. I thought that was a nice gesture.

I walked to the elevator whistling. Today was a good day.

Chapter 28

XAVIER

Call me Kunta Kinte!

I manned up and sucked up the pain. That crazy bitch fucked me up! It took every ounce of strength I could muster to free myself completely; sweat was streaming down my face. Each movement I made was pure torture. It took a good fifteen minutes to get out of the leg restraints. Pilar must have been a Girl Scout or something because she had those knots in there to stay. She definitely meant for my ass to not go anywhere.

I didn't even want to view the damage she had done to my face, inner thighs and chest. I reached down and checked out the merchandise; wanted to make sure it was still intact. If she had damaged that, she might as well have killed me because if she hadn't, I would most surely kill her. That's a fact.

One of the hardest things I ever had to do was to call up Dré to come pick me up at the hotel. What else was I going to do? In my most humiliating moment, I had to reach out to my best friend. I sure couldn't call up Kendall and have her pick me up. Pilar had taken all my clothes, including the robes from the room. She had even packed up every towel in the room. I was stranded with not a stitch of clothing and whipped up like some Kunta Kinte slave. Pilar made the New Orleans chick sound like a saint. Years from now, I might actually laugh at this entire ordeal. Probably not, but I might. I was in so much pain and at that moment, I didn't find one damn thing funny. Not a damn thing.

I heard a hard, frantic knock at the door. I went to answer it with the bed sheet wrapped securely around my torso. I noticed I was somewhat dizzy and felt slightly nauseated.

Dré hurried in looking concerned and ready to kick some ass. I hadn't told him much on the phone, other than I was in trouble and needed help. He came right away.

"Man, what's up?" he asked, looking around like he expected someone to jump out of the closet and attack. He definitely had his guard up. "Why you standing there looking like black Jesus?"

"You wouldn't believe it if I told you," I said, standing in the dark shadows of the room.

"Try," he said as he came in, sat down in a chair and gave me his full, undivided attention.

"What happened to your face? What's up with those scratches?" he asked, leaning in to examine them closely.

"Psycho Pilar fucked me up."

"What are you talking about? You still messing with that chick? I told you she was going to be your downfall. You just don't listen."

"If you saw the damage underneath this sheet, you wouldn't ask what I'm talking about."

I slowly lowered the sheet to reveal my chest and rewrapped it tightly around my waist.

"Damn!" Dré said. "Damn!"

I sat down on the edge of the bed.

"She fucked you up! Big time. You weren't lying. Damn!"

"Will you quit saying that?"

"Does it hurt?" he asked, standing to take a closer look.

"What do you think?"

"It probably isn't as bad as it looks. She barely broke the skin, but you should still get it checked out."

I dropped my head.

"What happened? I hope her pussy was well worth it."

I spent the next few minutes explaining what had gone down. He simply shook his head over and over again. Couldn't believe that shit. I almost couldn't believe it, and I was there.

"Dré, I'm serious. As before, it was like she became another person. One minute she was feeling me, we were getting our groove on, and the next, she became this demon from hell. When I came to, she was crying hysterically, mascara was smeared under her eyes, hair sticking out all over her head like Medusa, looked like a straight-out lunatic. She scared the shit out of me, man. I thought I had woke up to some horror movie."

"How did she knock you out? You are a big man."

"Hell, who are you asking? Probably gave me some type of a date rape drug. Put it in some wine she kept insisting I drink, now that I think about it."

"Damn. That's a bad-ass chick. Just you talking about her gave me bad vibes when you first mentioned her. She didn't sound totally there. The pieces were just not fitting. Even that discombobulated story about her suddenly appearing in Houston to work on a project. Yeah, right?"

"Well, you were definitely right. I should have listened with the head on my shoulders. So, you can say I told you so now."

I moaned in pain when I changed my position from my spot on the edge of the bed. I had taken a shower before Dré arrived and the sheer pain almost made me pass out, but I didn't want the smell of Pilar present on my body.

"Man, let's get you out of here and get you to an emergency room. Have you checked out."

"I don't know about that," I said, shaking my head.

"What do you mean you don't know?" he asked in disbelief.

"What will I tell them happened? How will I explain how I received these wounds?"

"I don't know. Tell them whatever. Tell them you were having rough sex. I don't know. You're the writer; come up with something creative."

"I guess I do need to get them checked. Wouldn't want them to become infected."

"Are you going to press charges against Pilar?"

"Hell, no! She is gone; went back to Georgia. My nightmare is over. I don't ever want to see that chick again as long as I live. Even then would be too soon."

I stood up slowly, like an old man.

"Hey, can you walk? Do you need my help?"

"Yes, I can walk," I growled, holding on to the wall.

Dré started laughing, slowly at first, then he was slumped over, holding his stomach because he was laughing so hard.

"I'm sorry, man, I can't help it. It's just the mere sight of you standing here looking . . ."

Another round of uncontrollable laughter burst forth. He was trying his best to contain it, but every time he thought he had it under control, another round would start.

"What would you tell the police? A psycho tied you up in a hotel room and beat the crap out of you with a leather whip."

"Dré, it's not funny. I'm in a lot of pain, man."

"I know you are, and we are going to get you to a hospital and fixed up. I'm sorry. However, you got to admit this is some hilarious shit. This sounds like a scene straight out of one of your novels. Some fatal attraction shit."

"I wish it were."

"And to think I thought the chick in New Orleans was crazy. If Psycho Pilar and Miss Voodoo Roots were sparred against each other, I wonder who would win. I'd bet on Psycho," Dré said.

Another round of laughter broke loose, and I couldn't say a

word because if roles were reversed and Dré were standing here looking pathetic and beat down, I'd be laughing my ass off too.

Thirty minutes later, I had managed to pull on the sweats, shirt, socks and sneakers Dré had brought with him, and we were en route to the emergency room of a nearby hospital. It's odd because as we made our way to his car, I had the strangest feeling we were being watched. The tiny hairs on the back of my neck stood up. I even looked behind and around me a couple of times, scoping out my surroundings. I jumped when a car blew its horn across the street. Pilar had screwed up my mind . . . I was acting paranoid. I jumped at every shadow and thought someone was watching me. Damn that Pilar. Damn! Damn! Damn!

Chapter 29

PILAR

People say I'm crazy, just a little touched.

I intensely watched Xavier exit the hotel and slowly climb into the car of a man I had seen him with a few times before. I can say that Xavier didn't look too happy. I assumed my little talk was effective, and I wondered how he was going to explain his injuries to Miss Kendall. I'd love to be a fly on the wall to hear that one. He was good at making up stories; after all, he was a writer, and she was naïve enough to believe them, so he'd probably be okay.

I trailed slowly behind Xavier and his friend in my car. I didn't get too close to be seen, but not far enough away to lose them. They never even looked back or noticed me. It was too easy. They appeared to be deep in conversation. I laughed to myself because I knew who and what the topic of conversation was.

I had hoped my little talk with Xavier would purge him from my system, but it didn't. I still craved him. I still wanted him and wanted him to want me. I was sorry I had to hurt him, but sometimes it took extreme measures to get extreme results. Maybe now, he would take me seriously. If not, I had other measures to take.

I followed Xavier and his friend long enough to see them pull into the emergency entrance of a local hospital. As Xavier was being helped out of the car, I sped away. He thought I was leaving Houston, but I wasn't going anywhere. And he couldn't make me. My mind was made up; I was staying right where I was—in Houston—with Xavier.

Earlier, as I had waited around to see what went down with Xavier, I had called Leeda. She seemed pleased to hear from me even though our last conversation hadn't ended on great terms.

"Hey, Pilar. It's good to hear from you. You've been on my mind a lot lately."

"How are you?" I asked. I sincerely cared about her.

"I'm fine. Can't complain. What's going on with you? Is Houston treating you okay?"

"No, not exactly."

"Really. What's going on?" she asked.

"I'm afraid I've been bad. Real evil."

"Oh, Pilar. What have you done?"

I broke down and told Leeda everything. From how horrible Xavier made me feel at times, treating me like a piece of meat, to how wonderful he made me feel at other times, to what I did to him at the hotel with the whip. I talked about how I loved him so much and I couldn't understand why he couldn't see that. Or maybe he did see it and didn't care. Maybe he treated me like he did because he could. Because I allowed it. Leeda didn't comment. She simply listened.

After I had purged myself, oddly I felt much much better. Sometimes, it was like Leeda was my priest at confession. She took all my sins and filed them away before they consumed me.

"Aren't you going to say anything?" I asked, waiting patiently for feedback.

"Pilar, there really isn't much for me to say. You've already done the deed. There's no taking it back. I hope you realize how much trouble you could be in because there are always consequences for our actions. Xavier could have you arrested for assault and battery."

"He won't," I said confidently.

"How do you know?"

"Because I know Xavier. I know what makes him tick. He'll take this to his grave; his huge male ego is wounded. Plus, he doesn't want to lose his fiancée and if she found out, he would most certainly lose her."

"Is that why you did this? So she'd find out?" Leeda said.

"No, because she will probably never find out. Xavier will protect her and their future lifestyle at all costs. She will be his trophy wife."

"Why, then?" Leeda asked slowly.

"Because I wanted to teach him a lesson. You can't play with my emotions and feelings like I don't have any. I wanted to get his attention."

"Do you think you got his attention?" she asked.

"Oh, you better believe it!" I started laughing. "I definitely got his attention."

"Pilar, listen to yourself. He was honest with you up front. I remember you telling me as much."

"By now, he should realize I'm the better choice for him. I can make him happy."

"You haven't made him happy. You've come into his life, disrupted it and caused him great pain."

"Well, he made me. He made me hurt him. He shouldn't have called me her name or said those hurtful things. He can be so mean and insensitive to anyone's needs but his own. Selfish bastard."

"Did hurting him make you feel any better? Did it take away your pain?"

"It did at the time, but now I don't feel anything."

"Now what?" Leeda asked.

"I don't know. I'm thinking about staying out here."

"Why? There's nothing there for you."

"Xavier's here. So, there is always hope."

"Oh, Pilar. Why do you keep torturing yourself like this? Why don't you come back to Atlanta where there are people who care about you and your well-being?"

"I don't know. I'll think about it."

"At least let me give you the name and phone number of one of my friends who lives in Houston. I've meant to do this before, but I always get distracted during our conversations."

"Leeda, I have to go."

"Wait. Hold up for a second."

"What? I really have to go."

"What about the phone number?"

"I'll get it later."

"Please don't do anything else that may get you in trouble. Please call me if you need me, because I'm here for you. Always."

"I won't do anything. I promise. I love Xavier. It's that Kendall I can't stand." With that I hung up.

It should have been her ass up in that hotel room being taught a lesson.

A few minutes later, I saw Xavier as he exited the hotel and I forgot all else. My single tunnel vision became Xavier. That was my reality. All else was forgotten . . . except for Xavier.

Chapter 30

XAVIER

I might open my eyes and find someone standing there.

I had good news and bad news. The good news was that I was going to live. The whip marks looked worse than they actually were. The doctor cleaned them up, gave me a prescription for an antibiotic and the pain and then sent me on my way. Didn't even question me too much about how I got my wounds. I guess they had seen some of everything, from gunshot wounds to you name it, working the night shift at an emergency room.

The bad news was that I was totally pissed. The more I thought about Pilar, the more I wanted to wrap my hands around her bony neck and squeeze. Squeeze until every ounce of life drained out of her. I wanted to hurt her and hurt her bad; make her suffer. I had never felt that sort of negative emotion about anyone before, and the depth of that scared me. If I saw her again, I wasn't sure what I'd do to her. I knew if I saw her that very moment, I would have to be restrained or I'd kill her. I can't even begin to explain the horrible scenarios that were going through my mind when I thought about Pilar.

On the other hand, my immediate worry at the moment was

how I was going to explain my injuries to Kendall. It was going to take some time for my wounds to heal, and she would immediately sense something was wrong if she didn't see me naked for the next two weeks or so.

I don't think I had gone two weeks without sex since I was a teenager. If you were my woman, then you best believe we were going to be intimate on a consistent basis. I knew men who married and then, a few years down the line, talked about how they received sex once a month or even less. Hell no! If you are my woman and you are lying in bed next to me, night after night, you are going to do something. But I realized I digressed . . .

I was racking my brain trying to come up with an explanation that Kendall would believe. As fate would have it, Kendall's and my schedules became so hectic that a few weeks came and went without us spending much time together. We'd meet and grab a quick bite during lunchtime or talk on the phone briefly, but there was never enough time to make love. So, it was never questioned and, in time, I healed. The scratches on my face, covered with a bandage, I explained them away by saying I had cut myself when I shaved.

Around the same time, I went out on the road to participate in a few literary events. Events I usually skipped, but they now gave me an excuse to be away from home. It was funny because I kept expecting Pilar to pop up at any one of my events acting like nothing had ever happened, like I had imagined that night. I even caught myself looking for her in the crowd, searching for that wild hair or seeing those doe-like eyes seeking me out during a presentation.

I had a few nightmares about her where I'd wake up in a cold sweat, my sheets drenched. It would take a few moments to realize I was only dreaming, so for a few precious seconds the terror would be real. Scared me to death. One very vivid nightmare was a repeat of the incident at the hotel. However, the ending was entirely different. This time, Pilar left carrying my dick and balls in her black tote. Right before she walked out the door, she smiled and said, "You won't be needing these anymore." It took me a couple of hours to fall back asleep after that one.

As more and more time passed, things eventually returned to normal, as normal as they would ever be, and I found myself letting my guard down. I guess Pilar really had forgotten about me and moved on. Thank God. I hadn't received any e-mails or any phone calls from her, so I was relieved that she had finally gotten me out of her deranged system. And I made a solemn promise to myself that my womanizing days were over. Pilar taught me a great lesson; one I would never forget.

When I went out to do a festival or other literary event, I did just that and resisted the urge to satisfy other needs. Of course, I was still propositioned by my female admirers, but I realized the love of my life was back home, waiting for my return. Kendall was enough for me, and I was happy. She wasn't a tiger in bed, but she had other qualities that outweighed that. Great sex wasn't everything. *Did I really just say that?*

Bottom line, Psycho Pilar was out of my life. I didn't know what happened to her and I didn't care. I assumed she was back in Atlanta, and I avoided Atlanta like the plague. I knew it was a major market for selling books, but I couldn't go back there, not yet. My publisher didn't like it, but what could they do? They couldn't force me to tour in Atlanta. That was just too close for comfort.

Life went on . . .

Chapter 31

PILAR

Revenge is sweet.

I had been in Houston for over a month since Lesson Night occurred. I decided to keep a low profile until emotions had time to heal. I continued to follow Xavier when he was in the city, and when he wasn't, I followed Kendall. I could tell Xavier had started to let his guard down, relaxing when he was out, because he didn't seem as jittery and didn't constantly look around or over his shoulder in search of some unknown threat.

Good. I wanted him to think his life had returned to normal. Not. Kendall, she was none the wiser. She didn't have a clue that I went through her discarded trash, spied on her at school, filled out credit card applications in her name and secretly hated her from a distance. I hated her with a major passion. With a passion so deep, it surprised me she never sensed my being. She was living the life I should be living, with the man I should be with. As long as she was with him, he'd never realize that.

Somehow, with all my extracurricular activities, I did manage to write a few articles for magazines and get paid. It didn't really matter. I could live for years and years off of the money I inherited. I wasn't in need of a dime as long as I didn't live beyond my means. Ironically, my mother ended up being more valuable to me dead than alive. I thought about her a lot—about how much I hated her.

Sometimes, when Xavier was out of town, I'd let myself into his house and sleep peacefully in his bed or sit for hours in his office. I would wear one of his button-down shirts from his huge walk-in closet because it still contained the slight smell of his cologne. I just wanted to be near him. Feel his presence.

One night, I sat in on an online chat sponsored by APOOO (A Place of Our Own), that he was doing while out of town. I signed in anonymously, on his PC, and asked him all types of questions. He had no clue who he was chatting with. He thought I was just another adoring fan. If only he knew.

During my downtime, I also researched the entire concept of a soul mate. I definitely thought Xavier was mine. The first moment I read his words, I felt an instant connection, an immediate bond, and when I met him at the book signing in Atlanta, I knew we had been together before. I was too familiar with him. I remembered his touch before he ever touched me. I missed him before I ever met him. An interesting article I found on the Internet, which summed up exactly how I felt, had the following to say about soul mates:

> Many theories exist as to what is a soul mate. The original roots of the concept go back to a belief in reincarnation. A soul mate is someone that you have encountered in many different lifetimes and have loved many times. That's why the first time you meet them in this lifetime, you feel as if you have known them forever before you even knew their name. There is a mystical déjà vu energy right from the start.
>
> It was originally believed that soul mates are created when

the creator takes a soul and splits it into two as it is cast into human form. Each half is supposed to learn the life lessons at their own pace. When the two halves sometimes cross paths during various lifetimes, they have a cosmic powerful bond because they really are of the same soul. They complete each other. They are often very much alike, and the intensity of the connection is too much for a mere human with emotions and issues to handle, so they painfully end up parting ways. When they both finish their lessons, they are both reunited in heaven and come together as a beautiful representation of love and unity. This is also known as your twin flame. Only one person is the other half of your soul.

Soon, not being able to see Xavier, eye-to-eye, face-to-face on a daily basis became too much for me to bear. I decided to reveal myself to him, and I decided to do it in a public place with Kendall by his side. The look on his face at that moment would be simply priceless.

I had followed Xavier as he made the trek from his home to pick up Kendall at her townhome. It was a Friday evening and, by now, the weather had a slight chill to it during the evening hours. Most people wore light sweaters. As they walked out to Xavier's car, arm in arm, they looked very much the part of loving couple. I watched them in disgust and disdain. Xavier opened the car door for her, just as he had done with me, and helped her in. He treated her like she was a fragile piece of expensive china. I wanted to break her into tiny pieces, sweep them up in a dustpan and toss them into the trash. He must have said something witty because she laughed, threw back her head, and caressed his cheek with the back of her hand before he closed the door. I couldn't stand her.

After Xavier was seated behind the wheel, they pulled off. I followed and watched them from a distance. I saw the light kisses he bestowed upon her lips at stoplights and how he carelessly ran his fingers through her hair. She leaned into him and they were very comfortable together. They couldn't seem to keep their hands off one another.

After driving for approximately five miles, they pulled into the parking lot of a seafood restaurant, parked and walked hand in hand the short distance to the front entrance. Xavier opened the door for Kendall and rubbed his large hand up and down her buttocks when he thought no one was watching. She laughed and slapped his hand away like a giggly teenager.

I waited a while before I ventured in. Even then, I was cautious as I made my way to the hostess who greeted me. I quickly determined where they were sitting. Hiding behind huge sunglasses and the pretense of reading a book, I waited until my table was available and made sure I had the waitress seat me far away from them. Once I was seated, I spotted them right away. I could watch them secretly without them being able to see me. Xavier and Kendall were seated at a booth, next to each other on the same side of the table. They chatted and had a grand ole time while they sipped drinks. I'm sure Xavier's drink of choice was a gin and tonic. Looked like miss golden girl, size 6 dripping wet, was drinking a cosmopolitan. Just the sight of them made me sick to my stomach. They made me want to vomit.

Xavier hadn't changed much. He was now sporting a goatee that was very attractive on him. Looked like he had buffed up even more. I had to shake off images of his bulging biceps expanding as he supported himself on the bed as he went up and down inside me. He was so fine. Too fine for his own good.

I had already devised a plan. I waited until they were in the midst of their meal before I made my move. I picked up my recently purchased copy of Xavier's book and headed their way. My first copy of his newest book was so tattered and well read that the pages were falling out. I wanted to slip up on them unannounced, with the element of surprise in my favor, but Xavier spoiled it for me.

He looked in my direction as I was about fifteen feet away. The look on his face went from shock to surprise, to anger to something unreadable. I simply smiled and put more strut into my walk. I knew I was looking good, smelling great and feeling wonderful. By the time I made it to their table, I think he had turned two shades lighter.

"Excuse me. I hate to bother you, but aren't you Xavier Preston?" I boldly asked, with a huge grin on my face, staring directly at Xavier.

"Yes," he mumbled, without breaking eye contact. Kendall smiled, eating another forkful of salad.

"I am your number one fan and I have all your books," I gushed excitedly. "Oh my God, Xavier Preston! Xavier Preston, I can't believe it!"

"Thank you," he stuttered, barely getting it out.

"It just so happens that I have a copy with me that I was reading during my dinner," I said, holding it up. "I realize you are eating, but could I bother you for an autograph?"

"No. This isn't a good time . . ."

"Sweetie, autograph her book. It will only take a moment," Kendall said, giving him a stern look.

"Pardon my manners. Hi, I'm Pilar," I stated, reaching out my hand to Kendall. She had one of those wimp-ass handshakes.

"Good to meet you. I'm Kendall. Xavier's fiancée."

"Oh, congratulations! You two make such an attractive couple."

"Thank you," she said, grinning from ear to ear like I had just told her she had won the million-dollar lottery.

"When is the wedding?" I asked. "Has a date been set?"

"Soon, we hope. We were going to wait until late next year, but we realized we can't wait that long to be together," Kendall shared.

Kendall and I turned to Xavier for comment.

"Can we, sweetie?" she asked.

"Huh? I'm sorry, what did you say?" Xavier asked.

"Sweetie, where is your mind tonight? I was just telling Pilar that we couldn't wait to make it official. I can't wait to become Mrs. Preston."

"Oh, how sweet," I said with as much excitement I could possibly muster.

I extended my book to Xavier and pulled a pen out of my black tote.

"Could you sign something like, to my number one fan, it was a pleasure meeting you. Love, Xavier," I put emphasis on the word *pleasure*.

I saw Xavier's jaw clench and unclench several times. I could tell it was taking every ounce of strength in him not to jump up from that table and strangle me. It amused me. Amused me a great deal.

When he handed my autographed book back, my finger touched his hand and he recoiled, tried to play it off by coughing into his closed fist.

"Thank you so much, Mr. Preston. It is such an honor to meet you. Could I ask one last favor? Could I please take a photo with you? My friends back in Atlanta will never believe I met you."

"Oh, are you from Atlanta?" Kendall asked.

"Yes, I am. However, I think Houston may become my permanent residence. The city has a lot to offer," I said sweetly and looked directly at Xavier.

"Well, I'm originally from outside Dallas, but I love Houston. If I hadn't moved to Houston, I would never have met Xavier."

I smiled.

"Sweetie, I'll take the photo of you two," Kendall said, standing up.

I reached into my black tote and dug around for my cell phone.

"Girl, I love that bag," Kendall noted, admiring it from a distance.

"Why, thank you. It was something I *whipped* out this morning before I left. It comes in handy; holds *everything* I need to handle business."

Out of the corner of my eye, I saw Xavier's jaw muscles tense up.

"You can take it on my phone," I stated, handing my cell to Kendall. "I have all sorts of memorable photos in there," I said, smiling knowingly at Xavier again.

He slowly stood up. I wrapped my arm securely around his waist. I could feel his body instantly stiffen as he tried to move away.

"Sweetie. It won't kill you to get a little closer," Kendall teased.

"Yes. Come closer. I don't bite," I kidded.

Xavier placed his hand firmly on the center of my back and didn't move. Didn't even smile. It was clear; he wanted this photo over with as quickly as possible.

As Kendall searched for the camera function, I whispered to him, "My panties are so wet."

"Excuse me?" Kendall asked, looking up.

"Oh, I asked did you get it yet."

"Here we go," she said. "Big smile, everybody."

I smiled. Xavier didn't.

"One more. Say cheese. Smile, Xavier," Kendall said.

"Again, thank you so much," I said, reaching for my phone. "This has been a thrill and I wish you both the very best. I hope you get everything, and I do mean everything, you deserve and that no one ever comes between you. True love is so hard to find nowadays. It shouldn't be taken for granted."

As I walked off, I could feel the sharp daggers in my back from Xavier's stare. Back at my table, I advised my waitress that I wasn't feeling well, paid for my cherry soda and quickly left.

By the time I pulled my car around and was headed out the parking lot, I saw Xavier as he ran my way. The expression on his face was not cute. He was not handsome when he was angry. I honked my horn twice and blew him a big kiss as I sped by.

Chapter 32

XAVIER

Catch me if you can.

Don't even ask me how I made it through the remainder of dinner. I was there physically, but my mind was all over the place. I couldn't recall the conversation Kendall and I had if my life depended upon it. I vaguely remember Kendall said that Pilar seemed to be very nice and sweet and I should take every opportunity to thank my readers for their support. I nodded, smiled and said the appropriate words at the appropriate times and somehow made it through dessert and coffee. Afterward, I feigned not feeling well, dropped Kendall off and made a quick exit. I didn't even go into her townhouse; just walked her to the front door.

I was numb; in complete and utter shock. If someone had asked me my name, I probably wouldn't have been able to tell him. When I first saw Pilar walking my way in the restaurant, I swore I was dreaming and tried to pinch myself to wake up. I thought I was having flashbacks from one of my nightmares. If I were white, I'm sure I would have turned a couple of shades whiter, been pale as a ghost, when I realized she was live, in living color and coming my way.

I couldn't believe that bitch had the audacity to walk up to me with my woman seated next to me and ask for an autograph. I had to give her props. She was bold. And extremely dangerous.

I had barely pulled off from Kendall's place before I dialed Dré's digits.

"Man, you aren't going to believe what just happened."

"Try me," Dré joked. "You won the lottery and are going to give me half."

"Man, be serious."

"Okay, what happened?"

"Kendall and I were chilling, eating dinner at Pappadeaux Restaurant, and Pilar strutted up to our table like she owned the place and asked for an autograph. Pretended like she had never met me."

"You're kidding, right?"

"I wish I were." I sighed.

"What did you do?"

"I signed the damn book and restrained myself from strangling her to death in front of a room full of witnesses, including Kendall."

"Man, you have yourself a certified stalker, and she ain't going nowhere soon."

I didn't say anything. I just massaged my forehead to ease some of the tension and took his words in.

"Are you still there?" Dré asked.

"Yeah, I'm here."

"You know I don't advocate violence against women, even though I know a few who need an old fashioned ass beating, but you are going to have to kick that bitch's ass. That is the only way she is going to get the picture through that thick skull and leave you the hell alone."

"I don't know. I've never put my hands on a woman like that before. I need to think this through first."

"What do you mean you don't know? It's going to have to be that or get a restraining order against her."

"I'm not sure about that either. I don't want to make this a big deal," I said, with exasperation creeping even further into my voice and mood.

"I think a woman whipping you like a slave has already made it a big deal," he volunteered. "What does she have to do next, brand her name on your chest in big, bold letters? Who knows what she is capable of? Do you really want to wake up one night with her standing over you with a butcher knife saying if she can't have you, no one can?"

"Thanks for the lovely picture you painted," I said sarcastically.

"Well, I'm sorry, I'm just keeping it real. You don't know what this chick might do next, and that makes her very dangerous."

"Don't you think I realize that? I guess I'm thinking about how I'm going to explain all this to Kendall."

"You mean she didn't say anything to her?"

"No. Pilar's intention was to toy with me, and I could tell she was getting great joy out of it, too. She had me exactly where she wanted me, and I couldn't say or do a damn thing about it."

"I hate to be the bearer of bad news, but it's just a matter of time, man."

"For what?"

"Before she sings like a canary to Kendall."

"You think?" I asked.

"Man, be for real. You know it's coming. That's why you have to make your move first. Beat her to the punch. Take some of the sting out of it."

"I'm going to L.A. in a couple of days to meet with my agent and a movie producer. I'll figure out something after that. I don't need this drama right now; I have to stay focused until then."

"That's right, my man is going Hollywood. Gonna see about making one of his books come to life on the big screen."

"We haven't gotten that far yet and we may never get there. This meeting is simply both sides coming to the table to do some preliminary talking. Do you know the percentage of books that get made into movies?" I asked. "And I'm not talking about independents."

"No. I don't," he said. "But I know you are going to inform me, Mr. Big Time Author."

"Very small."

"I have faith in you and your talent," Dré said. "Always have."

"I appreciate that, man. I really do."

"And I'm going to get through this mess with you as well. We've seen worse. If we survived our old neighborhood, you can definitely survive this. Keep your head up. This is just a stroll in the park," Dré said.

"Well, I'll let you go," I said.

"Just watch your back, man. Be careful and cautious. Be smart."

"I will."

"Keep your head up."

"When you return from L.A., you need to have a game plan in place. I'm going to get the name of a detective who can do some snooping around for you. You can't sit back and continue to be the prey; you've got to become the hunter."

Dré and I talked a few more minutes and then I hung up feeling a bit better. If nothing else, I knew my man had my back. He was like family. The drive back to my house seemed unusually long. I think I was subconsciously driving slower than normal because I wasn't looking forward to being alone tonight.

What if Pilar really did try to attack me while I slept? Sometimes, I could swear I smelled a woman's perfume in my bed, between my sheets, and it didn't belong to Kendall. I knew exactly what perfume Kendall wore because I purchased it. I would search for something in my office and find it somewhere entirely different from where I remembered putting it. Little things like that that weren't adding up had me thinking now.

I really didn't have a clue as to how I was going to get myself out of this mess. Not a clue. I was so lost in thought that when my cell phone rang, I absently picked it up without checking out the caller ID.

"Hey, babe. You got me so wet tonight that I creamed in my pants when you touched my back," she whispered seductively.

For a moment, I was caught off guard.

"What is it going to take for you to understand that I don't want your ass?" I screamed back.

"You don't mean that! Don't you want some more? I'm all wet for you. I need to feel you inside me. I'm burning up with desire, babe."

"I do mean it! You were just a booty call to me because you did all the nasty stuff my woman wouldn't. I could never be with you. Never! Men don't marry women like you. We just fuck you. You are nothing more to me than a good fuck!" I screamed into the phone.

"You will regret that! I promise you that," Pilar said in a voice so cold and sinister that it gave me chills. "And I keep my promises. But you know that already."

Click.

She hung up on me.

For the next two days, between looking over my shoulder and monitoring my phone calls, I somehow managed to stay focused on the task at hand, my important meeting in Los Angeles. I didn't hear back from Pilar after her threat, even though I now knew that didn't mean squat. I knew she was around. I sensed her.

My itinerary consisted of flying out to Los Angeles for the day, meeting with the producer, and flying back home the very next day. Los Angeles was not one of my favorite cities; I always found it to be fake and artificial. Everyone you met was an aspiring actor or actress, when I thought they were simply my waiter or waitress.

I was going to meet my agent, Douglas, and the producer, Robert, for lunch at some swanky Beverly Hills restaurant. We were going to discuss what both sides wanted in the deal and go from there. Kind of feel each other out. I couldn't even be happy for my opportunity because I still had my Houston problem. My problem was always in the deep recesses of my mind, never drifting completely away.

At the time, I didn't know my Houston problem would follow me out to Los Angeles.

The lunch meeting went well—much better than I expected. Conversation was kept casual and I received a good vibe from the producer. He was definitely interested, especially after witnessing the mega success of Tyler Perry movies at the box office. Douglas was kissing butt left and right, earning his fifteen percent. He was already picturing his new summer home and luxury car based on the percentage he'd make off a movie deal.

Douglas, Robert and myself were into dessert when I saw her coming. I froze like a deer caught in the bright headlights of a fast-approaching car. In my head, I heard myself repeating over and over again, *Be cool. Stay cool, Xavier. Just be cool. Relax.* I slowly lowered the steak knife I had lifted off the table without being aware of it.

Pilar waltzed up to the table like it was the most natural thing in the world for her to do. She leaned down and kissed me full on the lips. This chick was seriously toxic.

"Hey, babe. I guess I'm a little early." It took everything in me not to wipe where she'd kissed me.

I murmured something barely coherent and still hadn't moved an inch.

"Excuse my rude boyfriend. I'm Pilar. Xavier's girlfriend," she stated, extending her hand to Douglas and Robert. "We were

supposed to hook up after your meeting. He's taking me shopping on Rodeo Drive, and I guess I'm a little early because I'm
so excited."

She smiled. At that, they invited her to join us. Pilar was
totally charming. It took all my energy to stand up and allow
her to sit next to me. I could tell my agent was confused because he kept looking at me like he was silently asking *what the
hell is going on here?* However, he didn't want to say anything in
front of Robert that might place a strain on an otherwise perfect luncheon. Douglas knew I was engaged to be married; he
had met Kendall in the past. In fact, all three of us had gone
out to dinner once when he was in town.

Looking back, I don't know why I even allowed her to sit
down with us. Maybe I was in shock. Maybe I was in denial
that she was even there. For the life of me, I couldn't believe
she had the nerve to show up like that, in another city and
state, which further proved she stalked me. Maybe I didn't
want to cause a scene, which I knew she could do, and destroy
any chance at the deal. Whatever the reason, I didn't act and
Pilar took over, pulling my strings as puppet master, with me as
the puppet.

"Babe, I'm so proud of you," she stated, rubbing my back in
steady circular motions. *Stay cool. Be cool, Xavier. Just stay cool.*

Pilar grabbed my right hand and interlinked our fingers on
top of the table. Underneath the table, she discreetly placed
her other hand in my lap and proceeded to gently massage my
balls through my slacks.

"Are you okay, babe? You don't look too good."

I cleared my throat. "Yes. I'm fine." I picked up my water
glass and took a sip.

"Oh, I just love this man so much," she said, rubbing up and
down my arm.

"You guys give me hope," Robert said, smiling at Pilar and
back to me. "Love does still exist."

"We are living proof. I love you, Xavier," Pilar repeated, smiling.

Douglas and Robert amusedly watched the scene played out by Pilar and myself.

"Well, are you going to say it?" she asked.

"Say what?" I asked, looking confused. Inside I thought about how I wanted to smack that stupid smile off her lips.

"That you love me too."

There was silence. I had never wanted to hurt another human being so badly before in my entire life. I wanted to wrap my hands around that skinny little neck and just squeeze. Squeeze until every ounce of life was sucked out of her.

"Babe?"

I cleared my throat. I didn't think I could get the actual words to come out without vomiting, but then my dream of having my book made into a movie overrode everything. I couldn't stop the game that we played at this point.

"I."

"Well?" she said, looking at me with a smirk. "Don't be shy."

"I love you too, Pilar," I stuttered quietly.

"We can't hear you, babe."

I coughed, cleared my throat and took another sip of my water. "I love you too, Pilar."

Thankfully, my agent managed to get the conversation back on track and we finalized a date for another more formal meeting and wrapped things up for the day.

"Well, Mr. Preston, it has been a sincere pleasure meeting you and talking with you today, and I look forward to speaking with you in greater detail concerning our proposed project," he stated, standing to leave. "I hope we can work with each other in the near future." Douglas stood to walk him out.

"Same here," I stated, rising on wobbly legs to shake his hand in a firm grip.

"Pilar, good to meet you too. It's always a pleasure to meet a beautiful woman. Xavier is a lucky man, and he must bring you to New York with him the next time he visits. Perhaps my secretary can arrange to get two tickets to a Broadway play."

"Nice meeting you too. And that sounds wonderful. Doesn't it, babe?"

"Yes. Sounds wonderful," I mumbled.

I looked at her. Unbelievable. I couldn't see any beauty at that moment. Any beauty I had seen in the past had long since vanished into thin air, along with any common sense she had possessed.

Pilar smiled triumphantly in my direction and reached for my hand.

Just as Robert and Douglas were in the process of leaving, Pilar announced, "I'm going to run to the restroom, babe. I'll be right back." She kissed me on the lips, offering tongue. "I won't be long. Miss me."

When Douglas returned to the table, I informed him I'd explain what just happened at a later time. I was too emotionally drained to even begin to offer explanations. I knew he thought I was simply being a dog and Pilar was one of my women in L.A. By the time we finished up business-related issues some fifteen minutes later and parted ways, Pilar was nowhere to be found.

Believe me, I looked. I searched for her. High and low. I wanted to find her. Every fiber in my being wanted to find her. Oh, how I needed to find her. I knew she would make an appearance only when she wanted to be found.

Chapter 33

PILAR

These are my confessions.

Xavier was hardheaded. He still hadn't learned the lesson. He hadn't learned that he could not disrespect me and not have to pay the consequences. Sooner or later, everyone had to cash in their check. It was time for Xavier to get paid in full.

He had never dealt with a woman like me, one who didn't bow down and kiss his ass. He was used to women swooning over his good looks and charm. How dare he tell me I was just a booty call and he could never marry me? How dare he? After all I had done for him. How I went out of my way to please him. Went out of my way to make sure he was happy.

It was time to pay the piper!

Dressed in all black, from head to toe, with my hair neatly pulled back in a ponytail, I calmly walked the short distance from the sidewalk to the front door. I rang the doorbell twice and waited patiently. There was no need to rush. This would all be over very soon. I wanted to relish every second.

I knew someone was at home. From my position on the

street, I had watched the familiar car pull into the garage a few minutes earlier.

The door opened slightly and Kendall looked out with a curious expression on her face. She wore black skinny jeans and a cute red top.

"Hi," I said, taking a step forward. "I don't know if you remember me, but I'd like to talk with you for a minute concerning a personal matter, a common acquaintance. It's very important."

"You look so familiar; I never forget a face. Where do I know you from?" she asked, looking me up and down, racking her brain to come up with the answer.

"I'd like to talk to you about—"

"Oh, now I remember! You are the woman from the restaurant. The one who wanted an autograph from Xavier? One of his fans?"

I nodded.

Reality must have finally set in. "Wait a minute. Why are you here? How did you get my address? I don't understand," she said, taking a couple of steps backward.

"Everything will make sense in just a few minutes if you allow me to speak. It concerns Xavier."

She didn't move. Didn't blink an eye. It was as if she were frozen in place, like a statue.

"May I come in? I'll only take a moment of your time," I said again. "I promise."

"What is this about?" she asked, suddenly coming to her senses.

"It'll all make sense after you hear me out. May I?" I asked, gesturing toward the inside of her home.

Kendall sized me up for a few seconds and then opened her door just wide enough for me to step around her. She didn't waste any time with pleasantries as she walked toward the living room area and I followed close behind.

"What is this about?" she asked again, with her arms folded

defensively across her chest. She stood in the middle of the floor, while I sat on the sofa and made myself comfortable.

"It's about your man, your precious fiancé," I said coldly, not missing a beat. I had been waiting for this moment for months.

"What about him? How do you know Xavier other than from his novels?"

"I know more about Xavier than you think."

She didn't say anything, waited for me to continue.

"I hate to be the one to burst your naïve bubble, but I feel it is my duty as a woman to tell you the truth about the man who *claims* to love you so much." I emphasized the word *claims*. "Maybe then, you can take off those invisible rose-colored glasses you wear so well."

"And what is the truth?" she asked, half-laughingly. "What is so important that it would bring you to my home, invading my privacy?"

"Xavier and I have been having an affair for months now. I moved here from Atlanta to be near him. I love him. We are in love."

"I don't believe you," she said point blank, staring me down. "Now, you need to leave because I don't know, nor do I care, what games you are playing."

"You need to pull your head out of those books and wake up, college girl."

"How did you know I was in school?" she asked, her smugness now slowly vanishing.

"I know a lot about you, Kendall. More than you think. Xavier has told me all about you, usually as we were laying in bed after hot, steamy sex."

"You're lying. Xavier would never cheat on me. He loves me."

"I know you would like to think that, but deep down you know the truth. Open your eyes, girlfriend. Remember the night he went missing and you texted him?"

I knew I had hit a nerve because I saw the first sign of tears well up in her eyes. This would hurt now, but she'd thank me later. She didn't want to spend the rest of her life with a lying, cheating, no good dog like Xavier. Women didn't marry men like him; he was the type to have a good time with.

"Yeah, you remember. I thought you would. I don't know what he told you, but Xavier was with me all night."

"It was you who sent me that text?"

"I sucked his dick and he licked my kitty through the early morning hours. In fact, when your text came over, I had him in my mouth."

Kendall didn't say anything. She tried her best not to break down in front of me. She tried to be strong. She really did. I almost felt sorry for her. Almost. I knew from experience how loving the wrong man could hurt your soul. Make you feel like you were being held in captivity.

"Hmmm, he has the sweetest, biggest, juiciest black dick I have ever tasted." I pretended to shiver from just the mere memory.

"Oh, I forgot, he told me you don't suck dick. You think you are too high and mighty for that. Well, guess what? He likes it, so you'd better learn to love it, girlfriend."

Kendall finally found her voice. "Why are you doing this to me? Coming into my home and making up all these lies. I haven't done anything to you; I don't even know you."

"Little girl, I'm not doing anything to you. You need to ask your man that question. And you know I'm not lying. You know I'm not. I have no reason to lie."

"Get out!" she screamed, suddenly running toward her door, opening it wide.

"Don't you want to hear all the juicy details about how he simply adores eating my pussy? Said I had the best he ever had. We'd lay for hours in each other's arms while he stroked my hair and said he wished you were more like me."

"I don't want to hear this. Shut up! Shut up and get out!" she screamed, covering her ears with her hands.

"Why are you crying? I despise weak-ass women like you who sob like little babies when things don't go their way. Don't cry, get even," I said, slowly walking toward the open doorway. "I'm not your enemy. Your enemy lives over at 122 Main Street."

"Get the hell out! Now!"

"Plus, Xavier just loves to give it to me from behind. Has me on all fours and slowly eases inside me, takes his time, while he squeezes my breasts. He's so large, I can almost feel him in my stomach."

"Get out of my house! I'm not going to tell you again."

"And I love that sound he makes when he's coming."

"Okay, I'm calling the police," she stated, going for her phone on a small table near the door.

"No need. I'm leaving," I stated, walking halfway out. "I'm done here. Xavier is waiting for me."

Kendall stared me down with nothing but contempt in her eyes.

"Don't play the fool for Xavier, because Xavier only cares about Xavier. By the way, if you don't believe me, check out the little gift I left for you between the mattresses in his bedroom. You know the bedroom, the one with the massive bed. Does he have you doing all types of freaky tricks too?" I asked, enjoying every single moment of the scenario that was being played out.

I wanted to burst her perfect bubble and make her world come crashing down, down, down. I wanted her to experience what it felt like to experience pain and sorrow from someone you initially trusted and loved and to not have everything handed to her on a silver fucking platter. Oh yeah, I was love, love, loving this. Just the devastated look on her face brought me utter, complete joy. Then she slammed the door in my face.

I went ballistic. "Bitch, who the hell do you think you are? Don't you ever slam a goddamn door in my face!" I screamed, kicking the door several times with my foot, leaving dents, and pounding on it with my fists.

"You can run, but you can't hide, Kendall! I know where you live. You don't win, Kendall! Do you hear me? You don't get the man and live happily ever after."

With that, I turned, sashayed back to my car, whistling a tune from my childhood.

Your time is up, Xavier. Time to pay the piper.

Chapter 34

XAVIER

Nothing more to lose.

What's done in darkness always has a way of coming back around and biting you smack dead in the ass. That's what I'd always been told. The man who called himself my father, the one I saw maybe twice, three times a year until I was twelve, learned that the hard way. Mama told me a spurned husband arrived home a few hours earlier than expected and gunned him down. This man who called himself my father also told me women were placed on this earth for man's enjoyment and I should enjoy as many as possible. Yeah, what's done in darkness always had a way of coming out. Now, I had experienced it first-hand.

I had been back in town for a little over a week and had finally given Dré the go ahead to do what needed to be done, find a detective to track down Pilar. I realized I didn't even know the chick's last name. And I never asked. Looking back, I realized she never really gave up much personal info about herself. I simply dismissed it as her trying to be mysterious and alluring; now I think maybe she had something to hide. I didn't even know where she was living in Houston. We had always gone to hotels to get our freak on.

I couldn't believe I had been so damn stupid. Again, I was thinking with the wrong head. Never again. I had come outside the other morning with intentions to drive over to Starbucks to write for a while, and found all four of my tires slashed and my car keyed from front to back. Spray-painted on the hood, in red, was the word *WHORE*. Of course, I knew whose calling card that was. A couple of days later I received a delivery of a dozen long-stemmed black roses with a card attached: "I WARNED YOU NOT TO MESS WITH ME! I'M NOT THE ONE TO FUCK WITH! DO YOU BELIEVE ME NOW?"

Now, Pilar knew where I lived. Damn! Yeah, I was going to find her ass and beat some sense into her. Maybe Dré was right; that was the only way to deal with her. She didn't know who the hell she was messing with. I was through playing Mr. Nice Guy.

Before I could get the information from the detective, trouble came directly to me. I had just walked back upstairs from working out in my home gym, headed for the shower. I had my sweaty towel still wrapped around my neck and I hadn't bothered to put on a shirt. When I was stressed or frustrated, I worked out like a mad man. I had literally been working out each day for weeks now. I heard someone frantically ringing my doorbell, literally laying on it, and simultaneously knocking. I walked over and swung it open without thinking, annoyance and anger etched clearly on my face.

Before me stood a totally disheveled and obviously distraught Kendall. It appeared she had been crying for a while because her eyes were red, puffy and swollen. Her usually neat ponytail was unkempt and her hair was sticking up on the sides. She must have run out, because she didn't have on a jacket. What threw me was the pure hatred her eyes spewed my way. I wasn't used to that coming from Kendall. Before I could open my mouth to say a word, she slapped me hard across the cheek.

"How could you?" she screamed as she pummeled my naked chest with her bare fists.

I restrained her by the wrists, trying not to hurt her.

"Baby, baby, calm down. What are you talking about? What has gotten into you?"

"You know exactly what I'm talking about. Don't act dumb, Xavier. You slept with that bitch, didn't you?"

I hesitated for a moment, a moment too long.

"I knew it. I hate you so much!" she screamed, trying to get loose of my restraint. "I am such a fool. I really thought you were ready for love."

"Who—what are you talking about?" I asked, attempting to lead, half drag her to the living room sofa.

"Get your hands off me! Don't you ever touch me again!"

"Kendall, I'd never intentionally hurt you. Calm down. Talk to me without screaming."

"I can't believe I trusted you . . . loved you . . . gave myself to you and this . . . this is the thanks I get," she said, throwing up her hands.

"Baby, just calm down and let's discuss this rationally. What are you talking about?"

"What is there to discuss? The woman from the restaurant, your avid fan, your number one fan, you slept with her and moved her out here from Atlanta. To be closer to you."

"Who told you that?" I questioned.

"She did! After she paid an unannounced visit to my home and told me every disgusting detail of what the two of you did behind closed doors, behind my back. And then you came to my bed? Should I be tested for some disgusting disease you brought my way from your deranged lover?"

"Kendall . . ."

"How could you do those things to her? I thought you loved me?" she asked, hitting her chest.

"I do love you."

"No, you don't. You don't know the meaning of the word.

Out of all the big words you use in your novels, you don't know the meaning of a small one. You only love yourself."

I reached for her again. She frantically slapped my hands away.

"Leave me alone! Here, take your ring back too!" she screamed as she threw it in my face. "I could never marry a lying, conniving, cheating, untrustworthy man like yourself. Go back to your little groupie and have a wonderful life."

"Baby, I didn't sleep with Pilar. You have to believe me."

"How did she know about your bedroom and personal things about me? How do you remember her name from days ago if you've never met her before?"

"I don't know." As soon as the words were out of my mouth, I realized how ridiculous I sounded. My mind spun a mile a minute, trying to figure out a way to still get out of this mess. Dré had warned me that this day was coming; if only I had listened. I knew I had only a few more seconds to come up with a way to set things right again. For the life of me, I couldn't figure out how Pilar knew personal details of my bedroom either.

Kendall didn't say anything. She simply sobbed quietly.

"Okay, baby. I admit I had met her before, but I didn't . . ." At that moment, every ounce of strength drained out of her. Kendall's body went limp and I reached for her because I thought she'd fall to the floor in a heap.

"Don't . . . touch . . . me! Ever!" she said between clenched teeth.

"How can I prove to you that she's lying?"

"You want to prove it? Okay, I'll show you how!"

Kendall proceeded to run upstairs to my bedroom and I blindly followed, willing to do and say anything to make her believe me, trust me again. When Kendall reached my bed, she started fumbling underneath the mattresses, moved her hand back and forth, searching. Searching for what, I didn't know.

When she pulled out a pair of black, sexy woman's under-wear, I couldn't believe it.

"What is this, Xavier?" she asked, flinging them around my face. Finally, she threw them at me.

"I, I, Kendall, I can—"

"Save your breath, Xavier," she said, jogging down the stairs two at a time.

"I thought you were different from all the other men out there. When I met you, I thought we could create a wonderful life together, but I was so wrong. So freaking wrong. Stay out of my life, don't call me, don't come near me, Xavier. Leave me alone! We are over!"

When she reached the door, she turned and looked at me one last time.

"I loved you so much and thought you loved me back, but you threw it all away on a fling. I pity you. You are a man still playing boy's games. I hope she was worth it."

"Kendall?"

"Goodbye, Xavier."

Then she stormed out. She didn't look back.

With that, she was gone. Out of my life. For good.

I sat down at my kitchen table, with my head buried in my hands. Pilar had cost me everything. I had lost the one woman I truly loved. Deep down inside, I knew it was definitely over between us. There would be no winning Kendall back by apologizing and sending flowers, or wining and dining her. Kendall and I had discussed her trust issues many times. She didn't tolerate cheating—now or ever. She'd never be able to trust me again.

I sat at the table into early dawn and drowned my sorrows in a bottle of scotch I kept for special occasions. Sitting there, drinking straight from the bottle, my anger peaked. My hatred rose to the tenth degree. I saw red.

I regretted the moment I received that first e-mail from Pilar stating she was my #1 fan. Life is like that. There are moments when we look back and think if only I had done that or didn't do that. Well, I couldn't rewrite history. What was done was done. It was water under the bridge. I could handle the present situation, and I intended to do just that. Hell yeah, I was definitely going to handle this.

Chapter 35

PILAR

What's too painful to remember, we simply choose to forget.

I felt fabulous! Absolutely wonderful! This was what it felt like to float on cloud nine. Nothing or no one could ruin my good mood. Kendall was history, one less worry for me, and I was one step closer to winning Xavier over. I may not have won the war yet, but I definitely won that battle. Victory was mine.

I knew that both of them would hurt for a little while, but they'd survive. Kendall was pretty and smart; she'd find someone else, and Xavier would finally wake up and see clearly what I had to offer. They were bound to break up sooner or later because Xavier and I were destined to be together. I just sped things up a bit. One day Xavier would thank me.

I longed for a friend in Houston that I could celebrate my victory with and not one so far away in Atlanta. I'm sure Leeda would not be pleased with my actions anyway, so I didn't bother to call her. I could count on her to pull my happiness meter down when I shared my adventures.

See, I knew I didn't need to take that medication anymore. I was fine. Absolutely fine. I didn't like the way I felt or the person I became when I was on meds. I didn't have any emotion; I couldn't feel. It was like I was a walking zombie. Living life, but not really experiencing it. I wanted to feel. I thrived on emotions and feelings.

I stretched out on the sofa to relax for a moment because my confrontation with Kendall took more out of me than I realized. Before I knew it, I was knocked out for the count. I soon found myself caught up in another nightmare; they were occurring more frequently lately. This time, willing myself awake didn't work.

"*Pilar! Didn't you hear me calling you, girl? When I call your name, you'd better snap to it,*" *Mama said, standing in my bedroom doorway. She always appeared to consume whatever space she occupied. Bigger than life.*

"*No, ma'am. I didn't hear you,*" *I said with my head held down, staring at my feet. I really hadn't heard her because most of the time I was in my own little world, inside my mind. Daydreams filled my days.*

"*Give me that damn diary,*" *she screamed, snatching it from my hands. "I told you about wasting your time writing in this mess. What you thinking about that's so important you have to write it down? You better not have nothing in there about me or Daddy." Daddy is how she referred to my stepfather.*

I remained silent, still looking down at the floor. Mama started flipping the pages, laughing as she read one of my entries aloud, trying to talk like me.

"*A new boy named Marcus transferred to my middle school today. He is so cute and I wish he'd notice me.*

"*Girl, ain't no boy going to notice you. Look at you, all slumped over, a head full of tangled, unruly hair, big old eyes and you are not cute." She laughed smugly. "Ain't no boy going to look twice at you. Besides, you don't need to worry about no boys anyway when we have a man right here in this house."*

"*Can I please have my diary back?*" *I asked meekly.*

"Hell no! Did you not just hear me? You don't have anything worth writing about. Now get in the bedroom with Daddy."

I looked up in fear and my body instantly stiffened.

"The doctor said six weeks was enough time for you to heal," Mama stated. "It's been seven weeks."

"I don't feel good," I murmured.

"Girl, if you don't march your ass to that bedroom and handle your business. I've told you time and time again, everything comes with a price. Nothing in life is free. We are living in this big, fancy house with all our financial needs met. You'd better get your ass in there and do exactly what he tells you to do. If not, you'll have me to answer to, and we both know you don't want that."

I slowly rose from the chair at my desk with defeat in my every move. Each and every day I wondered why God placed me with this woman that called herself my mother. Why was I being punished? What did I do wrong besides being born? My life had been a living hell for as long as I could remember. Some days, I simply wanted to die. Most days, I felt like I was already dead. The walking dead.

"And, Pilar, you'd better remember to take those damn birth control pills every day. I'm not going to spend any more money for another abortion," she said, walking out.

I hate you! I hate you! For a moment I thought I had spoken out loud when Mama turned to look back at me.

The walk down the hallway was the longest ever. It had been seven weeks since I had participated in their sick games. My mama and stepfather were two of the most perverted people I knew.

I stuck my head in the door without saying anything, and didn't even pretend to be happy. He didn't care.

"There's my baby girl," he stated, pulling back the sheet to reveal his nakedness. "Look who has missed you. Come on in. Don't be frightened. You know I won't hurt you."

I walked farther into the bedroom, feeling totally powerless. There is no word in the world to describe being totally helpless, powerless as a child.

"Come on. You know what to do. Get over here and suck this dick. You know how I like that."

I walked over and proceeded to place the limp, wrinkled, sagging, disgusting piece in my mouth. When I looked towards the doorway, I saw Mama looking on like she was enjoying the scene played out before her. At least she didn't come over and join in as she sometimes did. I went to that other place in my mind to keep my sanity.

An hour later, I returned to my room to find the pages of my diary torn up, shredded and placed on top of the pillow on my bed. Powerless. Unloved. Unwanted. Those were three words that came to mind.

I woke up still sobbing. No one was ever going to make me feel powerless again.

Chapter 36

XAVIER

One flew over the cuckoo's nest.

About a week later, Dré came through for me. He called and gave me Pilar's home address. I knew the area and actually, it wasn't that far from where I lived. I hadn't told Dré what went down with Kendall and me. I had basically barricaded myself in my home, wrote when I could, exercised and drowned my sorrows in booze. When I wrote the address down on a notepad, I felt renewed anger, but most of all—powerful. I felt like I was in control again. I now had the upper hand. I was the hunter.

I waited until it was dark. Misdeeds went down easier under the cover of darkness.

It was easy finding her apartment complex.

I circled around a few times and spotted the car I had seen her driving before.

I parked, walked the flight of steps, found the apartment and knocked. Oddly, I felt very calm because I realized I was finally going to finish what I should have a long time ago. This bitch was going to get what was long overdue. It would all be over soon. That brought me peace.

No answer.

I knocked again, firmer this time.

"Pizza! Pizza delivery," I shouted and stepped out of the range of the peephole. I wanted the element of surprise on my side.

I heard someone moving around inside.

I knocked again. *Open the door, bitch.*

"Pizza," I said, trying to disguise my voice.

Pilar slowly opened the door as she was saying, "I didn't order a pizza." When she saw me standing there, time stood still for a few seconds. The hunter had now become the hunted. She was caught. She froze.

"I knew you'd find me sooner or later. Do I have your attention now?" she sneered and then had the nerve to laugh.

I lunged for her, kicking the door wide open. "Bitch, I am going to kick your fucking ass!"

She shrieked and ran just out of my reach. I calmly closed the door and locked it, took my time.

"Oh, no, don't run now. You are bold enough to step to me like a man, well, I'm going to treat you like one. I'm going to enjoy this."

I lunged for her and missed again. She fled around the other end of the sofa.

"Come here!" I screamed, grabbing at her as she ran near the kitchen table and chairs. I wasn't far behind.

Just as she tried to duck around to the other side of the sofa, I grabbed her by the tail of the short T-shirt she wore. Pilar looked shocked with her wild hair all in her face.

"Don't you ever go near Kendall again! Do you hear me?"

I held her by the tail of the shirt, and for a brief moment, I saw terror in her eyes, which quickly turned to something more sinister.

"Oh, did I make her cry?" She smiled sweetly, with us staring eye to eye. "Boo hoo, boo hoo."

Something overcame me. The audacity of her to stand there and mock me. I brought my outstretched hand back and hit her.

"You don't go near those I love!" I screamed, smacking her in the mouth. I split her lip and blood spurted out.

"Do you hear me? Kendall hasn't done anything to you. Stay away from her, bitch!"

I was so mad I was literally shaking. I don't think I had ever been that angry in my entire life.

Pilar wasn't fazed. She calmly touched her lip with her pinkie and proceeded to lick the blood off of her lips, then started laughing, this crazy hysterical laughter. I glared at her, stunned.

"Is that all you have? It's about time you manned up, you wimp-assed bitch," she challenged me, not backing down.

I slapped her harder this time, two times across the face. She slumped, then tumbled to the floor.

"Oh, babe, you are turning me on. Hit me again," she said, rising on one knee. "You know I love for you to punish me for being bad."

I grabbed a handful of her hair and pulled her face to mine as I leaned down. I knew I was hurting her because she was cringing. Good. I wanted her to feel pain.

"Bitch, for the last time, leave me alone. Keep your crazy, psycho ass away from me. If you come near me again, I will kill you." I threw her back on the floor. "Is that clear enough for you? Am I sending mixed signals now? Tell me what you don't understand."

"You like beating up on women, Xavier? Does that get you off?"

"I bet you have a hard on right now. Hit me again!"

I did as she requested; however, this time I didn't use my open hand. I used my fist, and this time she didn't get up from the floor. As she lifted her head to look at me, at first, all I could see was that wild hair covering her eyes. She reminded me of the character from the movie *The Grudge*. The one who came out of the TV. When she pulled her hair back with one hand, she looked absolutely looney with a split lip and swollen face. She started that unsettling, disturbing, hysterical laughter again.

Her laughter made me madder. I grabbed her by the shoulders and started shaking her. Tried to shake some sense into her. Her head kept bobbing back and forth.

"Stay away from me! Do you hear me? Stay away from me!"

The entire time, she was laughing. She pulled me down and we wound up tangled and rolling around on the carpet, struggling. I tried my best to get away from her clutches, and she tried her best to hold on for dear life. It was unbelievable; like I was caught up in some horror movie, fighting for my life.

I didn't realize she didn't have on any panties until she tried to place my hand between her legs. I was in shock, suspended in time for a few seconds. Pilar took that opportunity to kiss me, leaving behind a trail of blood on my lips. She licked it away.

"Hmmm."

"You are sick."

"What does that say about you?"

I shoved her away from me and she fell back, but recovered quickly. Her fingers were tangled in my zipper, unbuckling my pants, pulling my dick out. Before I could react, she had pulled me on top of her and her legs were spread.

I tried to pull away, push her back, but she had gained superwoman strength somehow. It was like she was high on some drug. She held on with a vengeance as she grabbed my dick and started to massage my balls. My pants were now down around my ankles, making me immobile. When I tried to get up, I stumbled.

I went off. I grabbed her hands and restrained them above her head and I was in her with one quick thrust.

"Is this what you want, bitch?" I asked, pounding into her with no mercy.

She tried to get away and cried out in pain. I pulled her back with my fingers, digging into her leg.

"Where are you going? Come back here. You are going to take this."

She struggled some more. We fought.

"You are going to leave me the fuck alone or I swear I will strangle the life out of you with my bare hands!" I screamed, with one hand around her neck and the other holding her hands down as I pounded away like there was no tomorrow.

"You like that? Yeah, this is what you wanted. This is what you can't get enough of. I'm going to tear your pussy up!"

I pumped her relentlessly. Over and over. I showed her not one ounce of mercy. I knew I was hurting her. I didn't care. Her pain was my joy. I spread her legs even wider. Wanted her to feel every inch of pain I offered.

"Oh, you are hurting me so good, babe," she moaned out of nowhere. I hadn't noticed that her eyes were closed and she was all into it now. "Ohhh, yessss!"

I stopped in mid-stroke. Here I thought I was doing some serious damage, and this psycho bitch was enjoying it. Licking her lips and softly moaning.

"Don't you dare stop," she screamed, with her eyes tightly closed. She was in ecstasy. "Make me come, babe. I'm almost there. Make me come."

"Oh my God, what am I doing? This isn't me. Oh my God." I tried to get away from her. Again, we rolled around until she somehow managed to get on top of me. Any energy I had earlier was totally depleted. I couldn't fight her anymore. She had won this battle.

"You are going to come for me," she screamed, repeating over and over as she rode me like a rodeo cowgirl, bouncing up and down, one hand held high in the air. "You know you can't get enough of my pussy." And I came. Came hard.

"That's right. Come in me," she said, laying her head on my chest. After my breathing subsided and I had the strength to move, I pushed her aside like a rag doll.

When I limped out the door with part of my shirt hanging out of my pants and the other half tucked in, trying to zip up my pants, the last memory I had of her was laying on the floor all beat up, her legs wide open, my come all over her, with her screaming.

I wanted to vomit. I was so ashamed of what had occurred. It was like we had played out some twisted scene in a porno/horror flick.

"Where are you going? Come back here!" she screamed. "Come back. Don't leave me. Please don't leave me, babe."

As I slowly stumbled down the steps, I heard her laughing that hysterical laugh again. Chill bumps raised up and down my arms.

"Xavier, come back. I told you you were going to love me!"

That laughter—laughter of the insane—followed me to my car and stayed in my mind and haunted me for years to come.

Chapter 37

PILAR

And I'm telling you, I'm not going . . . I don't wanna be free.

He loves me, he loves me not. He loves me, he loves me not. He loves me, he loves me not. He loves me not. He loves me not. He loves me not. Not! Not! Not!

I rocked back and forth, sitting cross-legged in the middle of the floor in my special room. Xavier looked down at me from hundreds upon hundreds of different angles. I had him plastered all over my walls; not an inch of space was bare. Even the ceiling was covered with photos of Xavier looking down at me from the heavens. I had made a special shrine of him from photos I had snapped when I followed him around doing his day-to-day activities.

There was Xavier in his front yard, doing some yard work. Xavier as he drank steamy hot coffee and wrote at Starbucks. Xavier as he ate lunch. Xavier caught deep in thought. Xavier as he looked sexy and fine as hell. Kendall was in some of the photos, but I had torn her head off or placed a big X over her face with a permanent black marker.

My special room, which was usually kept locked, was an extra bedroom that I had converted into a mini shrine. Some nights, I would sleep in there. Grab a pillow and lay on the floor, light some candles and look up at the many faces of Xavier. Hundreds and hundreds.

I had all of his books carefully displayed on bookstands that sat on a table covered with a pure white tablecloth. My first autographed copy was carefully wrapped in plastic. I even had mementos from our time together. A book of matches from the first restaurant we ate at, one of his pens, a towel from the hotel, a T-shirt taken from his house, a bottle of his cologne, a used condom: just items that made me feel closer to him.

Now, I had an ever-growing pile of shredded photos at my feet. On each *he loves me not*, I would shred another picture. This went on for hours.

I don't recall when I actually fell asleep. All I remember is waking up the next morning in the middle of the floor with caked blood and semen on my body. I was so stiff and achy I could barely move, let alone stand. Xavier did a number on me. I knew it could have been much worse if he had seriously wanted to hurt me with his six feet plus frame. I was in pain, but I also knew I'd survive. I had lived through much worse in my younger days. Much worse. Things that nightmares and horror movies were made of.

I walked into my bathroom like I was an eighty-year-old woman, slow and holding onto the walls. I ran a hot bubble bath, as hot as I could take it, with my favorite fragrance, and climbed in to soak some of my pain away. I must have lain there for over an hour before I moved again. By the time I stepped out and dried myself off, I had a plan in place. A brilliant one.

My busted lip and bruised body would heal in a few days, so I didn't have much time; I had to act fast. Time was of the essence. I was going to show him, once and for all. Xavier had the nerve to come up in my home and beat me. All he cared about was Miss Kendall. Every other sentence out of his mouth was about me leaving her alone. He didn't apologize. He didn't say the words I needed to hear. It was all about Kendall. Always about that damn Kendall.

Yeah, I'd show him. Once and for all.

I placed a quick call to the guy who had hooked me up with the keys to Xavier's house and given me the date rape drug. I needed yet another favor. This would be the last one. After tonight, I wouldn't need his services again. We discussed and planned. He agreed to meet me at my apartment at ten o'clock sharp.

I spent the remainder of the day preparing myself. I had to get the apartment in order so that it would all look like the real deal. I drank whiskey throughout the day to numb the pain and then I simply waited. Waited for hours, in the exact same spot, on my sofa. Sat in front of the TV without hearing or seeing a thing. I rocked back and forth and traveled to another place, another city, another age. Mothers are supposed to protect their babies. So much pain.

Anyone peeking in my window would have suspected I was in a trance as I rocked back and forth, chanting:

"He loves me, he loves me not. He loves me. He loves me not. He loves me not."

At ten o'clock on the dot, my contact arrived. I quickly ushered him in and closed the door. As agreed, he had on a dark hoodie that concealed his face.

"What happened to your face?" he asked.

"Nothing. I had an accident."

"Are you sure you want to go through with this?" he asked, looking around my ransacked apartment.

"Yes. Here's the money we agreed upon," I stated, handing him an envelope full of cash. "It's all there. Count it if you'd like."

"Naw, I trust you. I don't feel right about this with you being a woman and all," he stated, looking uneasy.

"A deal is a deal. You can't back down now. I need you."

"You must really hate this man."

I answered simply, "I do. I hate him now as much as I loved him once."

"What did he do to you?" he asked out of curiosity.

"Didn't love me back."

He stalled for more time. "Man, you jacked this place up. Damn, girl."

"Come on. You are wasting time. I don't have all night. Let's get this over with, and remember what I told you to do afterwards."

"I remember."

"Cool."

I took one last swig of whiskey. I braced myself.

The first punch clipped me in the face and I embraced it, because I knew when it was all said and done, it would serve its purpose. I embraced it.

"Stop, Xavier! Please stop," I screamed at the top of my lungs. "You're hurting me. Stop! Don't hit me again."

Fifteen long minutes later, dude had beaten the shit out of me. As agreed, I gave him fifteen minutes to leave. I timed it looking through half-swollen eyelids at my watch. Then I stumbled, half-crawled to my wide-open front door and knocked frantically on my neighbor's door. Miss Jackson, the one who came home promptly at 9:30 each night. I could set my watch to her.

"Help! Help me! My boyfriend, Xavier Preston, just beat me up."

The door opened to a middle-age face full of compassion and concern. The perfect nosy neighbor. The perfect witness.

"Call the police! Dial 911."

As she hurried away to call for help, it took everything in me not to let the smile that was playing at the corner of my lips escape.

Time to pay the piper!

Chapter 38

XAVIER

*F*ame costs.

The shit hit the fan! The police arrested me late Thursday night for assault and battery. I felt totally humiliated as the two burly officers, one black and one white, read me my rights and took me away in handcuffs. My nosy neighbors definitely got an eyeful and I knew I'd be the talk of the neighborhood over coffee the following morning.

Once I had been booked, with my one allowed phone call, I called Dré and briefed him on what had happened and asked him to retain an attorney for me. Unfortunately, nothing could be done until the next day. My night was spent in a dismal, grimy, pissy, foul-smelling holding cell along with other "innocent until proven guilty" men. They had us piled in there like animals; a few of my cellmates were sprawled out on the hard floor. As for these men who shared my space, lets just say I wouldn't want to meet them, alone, in a dark alley at night. I kept to myself as my anger grew. All I kept thinking about, besides killing Pilar, was those prison movies where they warn you against dropping the soap in the shower. I stayed awake for most of the night, watching my back and my ass.

I hoped and prayed that one day I'd look back on this situation and laugh, but the shit definitely wasn't funny now. Come to find out, not only did my arrest become the talk of the neighborhood, but became the topic of discussion on a national level as well. I don't know who leaked the story—I have my suspicions—but it was definitely leaked. Now, I was the talk of the country, by way of radio, TV and print media.

Authors rarely receive the type of publicity or uproar that other celebrity types have. After all, readers are interested in our novels and not who we're banging or what type of car we're driving or where we spent our last vacation. Most of the time, our faces aren't even recognizable. If we're good, our titles and names are known.

A-list authors can still go to the mall or a restaurant and not be bothered by adoring fans. Most of the writers I know are really very introverted people and shun the spotlight anyway.

Everyone from TV to magazine to newspaper wanted the scoop, the story—my stalker story. The press even reported that I was working on a book titled *Diary of a Stalker*. The more I thought about it, the entries I had been making for the last few weeks could turn into fascinating reading. Why not?

After I was released on my own recognizance, with instructions not to go within fifty feet of Pilar, who, I was informed, was in the local hospital because of her injuries, I worked at a feverish pace on my stalker tale. It consumed me.

Some people might have thought that this was taking self-promotion too far, when in reality, writing the book was my therapy. I had to do something to occupy my mind aside from the pending trial and spending countless hours with my attorney.

As for Pilar, I hadn't heard a peep from her. When I last saw her, she was bruised up in her apartment, but she certainly didn't need a hospital for any injuries I induced. Even though I wasn't supposed to, and I knew I was taking a huge risk, I drove by her apartment complex late one night. I was so bold as to go up-stairs with my baseball cap on and my head held down low.

Yeah, it was very foolish—but it was a chance I took. Any contact with Pilar could have put me back in jail until the ac-tual trial. When I turned the knob on the door, to my surprise, it was unlocked. Empty. Pilar was gone like a leaf in the wind.

I slowly drifted from room to room, and the only evidence I found that she had ever been there was a ripped photo lying on the countertop. It was a photo of me. I had no idea where or when she had taken it. Not a clue. That was the scary part.

I hadn't heard from Kendall either. I knew we were a done deal the second she walked out my front door. It made me wonder if our love was true, or if we were both searching for something in each other. If our love were true, would it really be that easy for her to walk away from me, without looking back once? Or if it were true, would I have gone back to Pilar's bed numerous times? What attracted me to her?

My mom and my man Dré called me every day to check on me and kept my spirits up. Dré came by most every weekend and hung out. I didn't go anywhere because my face was recog-nized now. I stayed in the house like a hermit and wrote to cleanse my soul.

Writing truly had a therapeutic affect. Seeing it in black and white was very sobering. I realized how I needed to grow up. I couldn't have my cake and eat it too. Life simply wasn't that accommodating. My mom used to say all the time, "If you play with fire, you are going to get burnt sooner or later." Pilar was my fire, my flaming inferno.

Pilar received her wish. Not a day went by that I didn't think of her. She was the first person I thought about when I woke up and the last person on my mind before I fell asleep each night. Even in sleep, she existed. She appeared in my nightmares larger than life.

This morning, I didn't bother to dress; I was doing a lot of

that lately. Dressing required too much energy. I was still walking around in boxer shorts with no shirt on. I had stayed up
last night, past three o'clock, working on my manuscript. It
was like I was obsessed with it; much like Pilar became obsessed with me.

I had recently grown a beard to try to keep people from rec-
ognizing me when I went out to run the few errands I had no
choice but to take care of. Sometimes, I received angry stares
or comments. It appeared everyone had chosen a side and
there were no in-betweens. People either sympathized with me
or hated me. I was either the victim or villain. There were
even some readers' groups circulating a petition around asking
readers to boycott my books because I advocated violence
against women. Bullshit. These people didn't know me. They
didn't know what went down. They weren't there. Every story
has three sides. My truth, her truth and the real truth.

The news media released sensational photos of Pilar looking
like her face had been run over by a train. CNN even ran the
story. I, of course, became the evil villain. Yeah, I beat her ass.
I admit it. She deserved it. I'm not going to apologize. But . . .
but I didn't jack her up like those photos were showing. I don't
care what she told the police; I didn't do that. I hit her with an
open hand. Only the last couple of hits were with my fists. An
open hand didn't do that type of damage.

I saw her at the preliminary hearing. Pilar, looking prim,
proper and wholesome, wouldn't even look in my direction,
refused to make eye contact. She made me invisible to her.
They presented evidence from the photos taken the night of
the incident, supposedly had witnesses in the form of her neighbors, who saw me fleeing the scene. It was all surreal.

Pilar did something that completely surprised us all—she
refused to press charges. She retracted everything. She even
detailed how she paid a thug to beat her up. However, the state
of Texas had other plans and decided to proceed. There was

enough evidence against me for the original assault and battery charges.

It was around noon as I made my way to the mailbox. That was my highlight of the day. My walk to the mailbox. Halfway there, my phone rang.

"Hey, man."

"Hey, Dré."

"What's up?" he asked.

"The usual."

"That means you are writing or taking a break from writing," he said.

I had to laugh a little, and laughter was not something I did lately. He was right; I was always passionate about my craft. After all, it paid my bills and kept my lights on, but now I was consumed by it.

"You got it."

"You want to go grab a few beers later?"

"No. I'll pass."

"Man, you have to get out of that house. You are making yourself a prisoner in your own home. You can't continue to live like that."

"No. I'm cool."

He sighed.

"I'm worried about you."

"Don't be. Remember, I'm a survivor. This is just a stroll in the park."

There was silence.

"Do you ever think about all the signs that were there?"

"Every minute of every day," I said.

"I can't believe things got so out of control."

"Me neither, man. Me neither," I said, standing in my driveway.

"The news reports talk—"

I interrupted. "You mean the *entertainment* reports?"
Dré chuckled.

"Yeah. They talk about you and Pilar, revealing your lives to
the world. Trying to spin public opinion. Using phrases like
author's alleged stalker tale like you made that shit up—and re-
ferring to Pilar as *abused and discarded by ex-lover*. I found myself defending you to some of my co-workers the other day,
telling them you aren't like the media portrays you to be and
they shouldn't believe everything they read or hear."

"I can't watch TV anymore. It's amazing how they twist and
fabricate statements to fit their agenda."

"I feel you."

"They even showed Kendall with her new man, dining at a
local restaurant," I said. "She looked happy."

"Man, you'll find someone else."

"Right now that is the furthest thing from my mind. I'm just
trying to keep my black ass out of jail."

"You will. You have the best attorney money can buy. You'll
win this. Have faith."

"I hope so. I truly hope so, man."

"Anyway, as I was saying, they make Pilar out to be an angel.
Like she is some upstanding citizen that you took advantage
of."

I got quiet. Lost in thought. Lately, I found myself more in-
trospective. I couldn't believe this nightmare I was living was
my life. My life flashed across media channels for the entire
world to see and dissect. Tune in at six and eleven o'clock for
the latest updates. I was about to lose everything I had worked
so hard to build; all over a piece of ass. I realized I couldn't
blame anyone but myself for my predicament because I had
made the stupid mistake of bringing that bitch into my life.
Now, I was picking up the pieces and barely holding on.

"You there?" he asked.

"Yeah, I'm here."

"Listen, try to drop by the spot. Drinks are on me."

"We'll see."

"Hang in there, man. You'll survive this."

We hung up.

I continued my walk to my brick-encased mailbox and pulled out mostly bills and advertisement for some product or service I didn't need or desire. There was an official-looking envelope with a postmarked address I wasn't familiar with. I absentmindedly walked back to the house and started to rip it open. Any other day, I would have noticed the beauty of the day, but lately I didn't see beauty, only pain and the ugliness in people, including myself.

Once I got inside, poured myself some orange juice from the refrigerator, I finally focused on the envelope. It contained a letter.

Mr. Xavier Preston,

It is with considerable thought and introspection that I've penned this letter to you. What I'm about to tell you is of a confidential nature, told firsthand to me. However, I feel this is information you should be privy to. Maybe it will shed light on some of the unanswered questions I'm sure you must have. Possibly it can provide some sort of closure, at least at some level. Do with it what you will, but if I'm questioned, I will deny the existence of these statements.

Like the rest of the nation, I feel as if I know you personally. I've watched your tragedy unfold like a daytime soap opera or reality show as the nation hangs on every episode. I can't help but think I could have prevented some of what has occurred. Guilt lays heavy on my heart. Yet, I am bound by professional codes of conduct.

You see, I was Pilar's psychiatrist for many years, over eight to be exact, before she convinced herself she was well and dismissed me. As I'm sure you know by now, Pilar is a very sick woman. Yet, she has the ability to function or appear normal in society, when she takes her meds and isn't severely stressed.

As I've stated, I know Pilar very well and I realize what she is capable of. And I believe you. I do not believe she was your mistress or any of the other misinformation that has been widely reported or circulated in the media. However, I hate that you felt it was necessary to take matters into your own hands, literally. That was an unfortunate mistake.

Yet, I feel for Pilar as well, and I have grown to love her as a daughter. I want to protect her and guide her because she is simply yearning for love—the love she never received as a child. After I moved my practice to Atlanta, I remained in contact with her, not as her doctor, but as a friend and confidante over the years.

Pilar was severely abused as a child by her mother and step-father. One of the worst cases I've ever seen. I can't begin to detail the atrocities that were bestowed upon her by her own mother. Things were done to her that a child should never have to endure. I'm not sure if most adults could endure them. Pilar turned inward to survive. She would take herself to another place—within her own mind. There, she was safe and protected and loved. For most of her adult life, she has been searching for that missing love and for someone to protect her. She hasn't found it yet. You are her type: tall, physically fit, overpowering, aggressive, direct.

There was only one time in which she felt the love and kindness of another human being; that was when she briefly lived with an aunt when her mother was incarcerated for drug trafficking. However, her beloved aunt died of ovarian cancer. She inherited property and money from the death, and it was placed in trust until she reached adulthood. From this, Pilar learned a lesson—love is fleeting. You have to hold on to it when you find it. Hold on to it with all you have. By any means necessary.

This has been a constant pattern in her life. Her love turns into obsession. There have been unexplained incidents that have plagued and followed her as well. Her mother and her stepfather were mysteriously killed in a house fire, but authorities could never prove it was intentionally set. Because of that, Pilar inherited a large sum of money, mainly because of her mother's husband, who also shared a bed with Pilar. Later, a boyfriend who was breaking up with her and who had been abusive to her mysteriously committed suicide. They found him with a bullet in his head. Authorities never found out what actually happened. To this day, his relatives do not believe he killed himself. You can form your own conclusions, but tragedy appears to follow Pilar.

I'm not trying to condone her actions, but mainly explain why she is like she is. Pilar is not a monster. She is simply a confused, hurt little girl living inside a woman's body, searching for the love she never had. She thought she loved you, Mr. Preston. Yes, she spoke highly of you in the beginning. You treated her with kindness, initially. You see, she confuses sex with love, and I feel you took advantage of that.

When you rejected her, you represented all the others who had mistreated her as a child. Then, she stopped taking her medication, and events spiraled tragically out of control. I hope this explains Pilar on a deeper level, and even though her actions were terribly wrong, at least you can understand why she acted as she did. She's not the monster you think she is. Pilar's sickness is the monster.

Sincerely,
Leeda Smith, PhD

Chapter 39

XAVIER

One year later

When the verdict was read in the courtroom, I sent a quick prayer of thanks straight to God. I had my life back. I got off with five years of probation and community service. My life quickly returned to normal—as normal as it would ever be. With the verdict, the media finally left me alone, since I was now old news.

My novel, *Diary of a Stalker,* was released and became an instant hit. It is my best-selling book to date and has gone through several print runs, selling millions of copies and translated into many languages.

I didn't get the movie deal I desired, at least not for the book I wanted, but *Diary of a Stalker* is being made into a movie. I've moved out to Los Angeles, temporarily, until the movie is completed. They have just started filming, but it has been quite an experience so far. I wouldn't sign the contract unless I was given free access to input my thoughts as a creative advisor. I didn't want some Hollywood writer rewriting my words or intent.

The first day I walked on the set, I almost freaked when I

saw the actress who was to play Pilar. She had that same wild, crazy hair, big doe-like eyes, and the resemblance was absolutely uncanny.

The last contact I had with the real Pilar was a few days after my trial ended, over a year ago. I came home to find the following e-mail:

Hey, babe,

I watched the news and heard when the verdict was handed down. Good for you. I'm so happy you got off with a light sentence. I want you to know that I've forgiven you and I wish you nothing but love, joy and happiness.

I've thought about you lately and how wonderful we could have been together. I can hear you now; you don't live for woulda, coulda, shoulda. We were definitely good for each other between the sheets. You'll never find anyone who is willing to give herself so freely and unselfishly to you as I was. I loved you so much and still do, but I finally realized I couldn't make you love me back.

As much as you claim to know about women and relationships, I realize you were not ready for a woman like me. I was ready for love, all the joy and the pain, and you were simply running. You still have a lot of growing up to do in the relationship department. Address your intimacy issues before they come back to bite you again. As for me, I have all the time in the world. I can wait. I feel our paths will cross again some day.

Some nights I crave you so much, just a simple touch. I miss you so much! Do you miss me?

Loving you now and always,
Pilar

That was the e-mail. What can I say? It is what it is. I've accepted my part in the events that transpired. I was not blameless by any means, and I don't make myself out to be. I hope I've learned some valuable lessons in dealing with women and my treatment of them. I've made many mistakes and hurt people in the process. However, I can't continue to beat myself up, nor live the rest of my life looking over my shoulder. Life goes on.

Yes. That's the bottom line: Life goes on, and I intend to experience as much of it as I can while I can. I've always heard that the making of a good writer is one with rich life experience, and I have many more stories to tell. Some day, I know I'll write the ending to Xavier and Pilar's story, because I have a strong feeling it's not finished yet.

Chapter 40

PILAR

A year later

I had to get away, away from the States. I had spent the last year on a tropical island, enjoying the beauty and joy of life and forgetting about Xavier. Hey, if he didn't realize a good woman when he saw her, then that's his loss. One day our paths will cross again. . . . It's our destiny.

Waking up to an ocean right outside my door, eating healthy and not experiencing the hectic lifestyle of most Americans had been therapeutic.

I read where his precious Kendall moved on. Saw a write-up in the society column in some magazine about her pending marriage to a doctor, a surgeon, at that. That gave me hope for finding love. I know my soul mate is out there somewhere and I intend to find him even if it kills me.

I'm back in the States now. I stepped off a plane in Los Angeles a month ago. I didn't know what to do with myself. On impulse, I sent in my resume for an opening at a local newspaper; a position as a reporter. Well, I received a job offer and accepted. When the editor walked me around the office, introducing me to everyone, I was so excited. I just knew something wonderful was going to come out of the experience. It was time for a new beginning, a new start.

It was going to be great to work around people again. Leeda had suggested I get back out in the workplace, as opposed to working freelance from home. Working from home was a very lonely existence, but she wasn't too thrilled to learn of my plans to live in L.A.

Anyway, I digress. When the editor took me into the office of the business manager, I literally lost my breath. The man standing before me was simply gorgeous, all six feet plus inches of his red-bone complexion with hazel green eyes. He smiled. He had a beautiful smile. Gorgeous teeth. Big feet.

When we shook hands, I instantly felt an attraction. I felt sparks go up and down my arm and my pussy twitched. Something told me we would get to know each other very well before it was all said and done.

"Hi, I'm Pilar," I stated, smiling sweetly.

QUESTIONS FOR DISCUSSION

1. Do you think groupies exist in the literary world?

2. Did Xavier take advantage of Pilar in the beginning of their relationship?

3. What are your feelings regarding Pilar? Did you like/dislike her? Did you feel sorry for her?

4. What are your feelings regarding Xavier? Did you like/dislike him? Do you know men like him?

5. Do you feel Xavier's womanizing ways were a by-product of his upbringing?

6. Why do you feel Xavier continued to sleep with Pilar *after* experiencing some of her irrational behavior?

7. Did Xavier get what he deserved? Why or why not?

8. Could Pilar have overcome her past?

9. Did Pilar learn anything by the end of the book? Did Xavier?

10. Have you ever been stalked? Have you ever stalked anyone?

11. In the electronic era, do you think excessive e-mailing is a form of stalking? What about keeping up with someone

from an online site such as MySpace, Facebook or Twitter?

12. Had you figured out who Leeda was?

13. What was your favorite scene from *Diary of a Stalker*?

14. Do you feel Xavier has seen the last of Pilar?